# The Rains of Hamakua

# The Rains
## –of–
# Hamakua

# Stacie Macias

**AVALON BOOKS**
THOMAS BOUREGY AND COMPANY, INC.
401 LAFAYETTE STREET
NEW YORK, NEW YORK 10003

PRINTED IN THE UNITED STATES OF AMERICA
ON ACID-FREE PAPER
BY HADDON CRAFTSMEN, SCRANTON, PENNSYLVANIA

For my husband, Russ Macias, whose love lights my way

*Chapter One*

On her first day in Hawaii, during a long walk, Leigh Christie came upon the cemetery.

Actually, it was a family plot, for only seven granite headstones stood among the ferns alongside the red dirt road, and all of them, either through birth or marriage, bore the name Akina. They were large and deeply carved with square lettering. In the dappled green shade of the overhanging trees, Leigh knelt and looked at the largest of them.

It was a double headstone carved in the shape of an open book. It read, *Here lies Lino Akina, descendant of the first Hawaiians from Tahiti. Beloved wife Noelani Beck Akina, granddaughter of missionary Augustus Beck. Rest in Peace.*

Other Akinas clustered around them—*David Akina, son of Lino and Noelani; Mei Ling, wife of David; Lani, beloved daughter; Paolo, devoted husband.* A fern frond obscured the writing on the last grave.

Leigh crept over and moved the frond aside. Moekane Akina. He had died less than twenty-seven years before.

''He was my uncle,'' a voice said.

1

Leigh vaulted to her feet and spun around. *He's found me,* she thought. Somehow, Malcolm had tracked her down.

It had begun on the plane. She had not even noticed him on the long flight across the Pacific. But when Aunt Florence left her seat to use the rest room a few minutes before they were due in to Hilo, Leigh saw him there, in the aisle seat, reading a college horticulture textbook. He was a young man of Asian descent, nice-looking, in his early thirties, with a dark, ruddy complexion that spoke of a life spent largely outdoors. On the wrist closest to Leigh he wore an expensive-looking gold watch. Nothing about him was the least unsettling. Not yet.

He noticed her attention to his watch and raised his wrist to look at it. "It's still on Los Angeles time," he said, and began to adjust it. "I'm coming back from visiting my mother."

"You live in Hawaii?"

"Yes. Are you on vacation?"

"Yes—my first in four years. I'm overdue. I'm traveling with my aunt, so I'm sure I'll get plenty of rest."

"Well, here's to a relaxing vacation—Leigh? That is your name, right?"

"How did you know that?"

His smile was a bit smug. "I heard your aunt talking to you a while ago. My name is Malcolm." He closed the horticulture textbook. "I'm surprised you're flying to the Big Island. Most vacationers go straight to Honolulu."

"We're staying with a friend of my aunt's. He owns an estate in Huma—Huma—"

"Hamakua."

"Yes. You know it?"

He gave her an odd smile. "Yes. I know it."

There was something a little strange about him. She returned his smile uncertainly and allowed the conversation to trail off, turning to take the in-flight magazine from the pouch in front of her. Inside was an article about Hawaii's coral jewelry. Before they left Los Angeles, Aunt Florence had said that she wanted to shop for a necklace of corals. Leigh would have to show her this article.

If she ever came back to her seat. Apparently she had struck up a conversation with someone on the way back from the rest room and had decided to sit with her for a while. Leigh could see her aunt's smart red Oleg Cassini hat bobbing as she talked. Aunt Florence would not be returning soon.

Leigh flipped another page of the magazine. The page caught on the craggy stone of the pendant she wore around her neck and ripped. Impatiently, she freed the page and smoothed it out. She held up the pendant and looked at it.

Aunt Florence had given it to her just before they boarded the plane in Los Angeles. She had acquired it on her first trip to Hawaii, she said, and now she wanted Leigh to have it. Leigh had smiled tightly and allowed Aunt Florence to put it around her neck. The craggy, rough stone was olivine.

But it was not the shiny, clear green olivine that Leigh had seen before. This simply looked like a gray rock shot through with streaks of dull green. It was the ugliest piece of jewelry Leigh had ever seen, but she couldn't hurt Aunt Florence's feelings. She would wear it until they got to their bungalow on the estate, and then hide it away in her luggage and hope Aunt Florence wouldn't think of it again. She only wondered how a woman of her aunt's impeccable taste could have chosen such a horrible piece of jewelry.

Leigh turned it over and looked at the smooth gold back. *Souza—Oahu* was etched in the gold. If Leigh had owned that store, she would have thought twice about taking credit for this particular piece of merchandise.

The speakers overhead crackled to life to announce that they were beginning their descent toward the Big Island of Hawaii. Excited, Leigh leaned forward to look out the window. A strand of her waist-length brown hair fell over her shoulder and she pushed it back automatically.

The clouds separated and there it was—a rocky coastline of black and red earth clothed in riotous green vegetation. Beyond the rugged coastline were the patchwork rectangles of crops, from pale to dark green, separated by long gashes of red earth.

There was a sudden jerk on the pendant that dangled around her neck. Leigh gasped and whirled. Malcolm was grasping the pendant, pulling her with it. His eyes were wide.

"What do you think you're—" Leigh began.

"Where did you get this?" he demanded.

For a moment she was too startled to speak. Then indignant anger rushed through her and she pulled the pendant away from him and tucked it inside her blouse. "None of your business!" She could feel her heart pounding wildly with fear and anger. "What's the matter with you, anyway?"

Abruptly, he sat back in his seat and lowered his eyes. "Nothing. I'm sorry."

Leigh stared at him. She expected him to offer some sort of explanation, but he merely opened his horticulture textbook and began to read again.

He did not look at her again until the landing gear touched down on the runway and the retrojets fired up. Then it was merely a flicker of a look as he bent down to retrieve his shoulder bag from under the seat. They did not speak again.

Leigh and her aunt were met at the airport in Hilo by George Honua, a young Hawaiian man who worked for Simon Trowbridge. Simon was a fellow attorney of Aunt Florence's late husband and their host for the next four weeks. He owned an estate, Wailani, and a small but prosperous sugar plantation on Hawaii's Hamakua coast. George packed Leigh and Florence and their luggage into his Jeep and drove them north from Hilo along the black-and-turquoise coast.

The Hamakua coast was a series of deep valleys, each a small world in itself. Waterfalls cascaded down green cliffs to streams that ran out to sea through sugarcane and taro fields.

They turned off the highway onto a road that wound down into one of these valleys. Honola'i, the valley of tranquillity.

The valley spread out below them, blurred in veils

of watercolor mist as the sun drew moisture from the earth. The arms of the valley stretched out to the sea to cradle the pure blue water in a long curve of black sand and lava rock. Sunlight dazzled off the bay. Leigh had never seen anything so beautiful.

"This valley was created a long time ago, when lava from Mauna Kea flowed down its slopes to meet the sea," George said. "When the hot lava hit the cold waves of the Pacific, it exploded into millions of tiny bits. That's why the sand on our beaches is black, not white."

He guided the Jeep around a hairpin turn through an overhang of tropical trees with wild orchids dripping from their branches, and out again into the sunlight.

"Down there is Simon's house," George said, pointing. "At the top of that little hill. You can just see it through the trees."

Leigh saw a flash of a veranda and large glass windows before the trees obscured the view. They wound their way down to the floor of the valley and turned toward the ocean. Now and then they passed a house nestled among palms and banana and plumeria trees.

"Here's the general store," he said. "You probably won't need anything while you're here that Simon can't get for you, but if you do, the store is close enough to walk to."

Leigh glanced out the window at the palm-thatched wooden building George indicated. Above the veranda was a sign that read, AKINA'S GENERAL STORE.

Half a mile farther, George turned left onto a road that was not much more than a path. At the mouth of this road was a small, unpretentious sign—WAILANI. They had just crossed onto Simon Trowbridge's estate.

George pulled up in front of a brown-and-white wooden bungalow, sheltered in the green shade of a banyan tree. The house was on stilts, which were concealed by a skirt of lattice. Wooden stairs and a bannister led up to a veranda that ran the length of the house. All the windows were covered with weathered white shutters. At the far corner of the veranda grew a plumeria tree, heavy with yellow-centered white blossoms.

George took them up to the veranda and unlocked the front door. From the veranda Leigh had a clear view of the ocean through a stand of low trees.

"Is there a beach down there?" she asked George. "Or is it all rocks?"

"There's a beach. Black sand."

"Oh, that's right! This is where the lava exploded."

George laughed. "You remembered! Just follow the path down the slope after you cross the road. But don't go too far out into the water. The waves can get rough and there are lava rocks underwater. They can rip you up pretty bad."

"Then I definitely won't go out too far."

His smile was a flash of white teeth in his deeply tanned face. Friendliness danced in his marble-brown eyes. "Good. Oh, and something else you should watch out for—something even more dangerous than the rocks."

"What?"

"The local boys. Don't be surprised if you find

yourself being watched. There hasn't been a beautiful *haole* girl down here in a long time.''

''What's a howlie?''

George shook his head. ''*Haole*. That's the Hawaiian word for white people. Originally the word meant 'foreigner,' but since the first foreigners the Hawaiians saw were Captain Cook and his English crew, it's come to mean whites. So you're a *haole*. And a beautiful one, like I said, so don't be surprised if you get the eye from a few of the local guys.''

They went inside the bungalow. A small front room greeted them, furnished with rattan chairs and tables. There was a kitchen, a bathroom, and two bedrooms, one fairly spacious, the other little more than a cubbyhole. Leigh knew which room she would take. Aunt Florence couldn't stand cramped quarters. Besides, she had twice as much luggage.

Leigh went into her bedroom while George got their bags. The shutters were closed over both windows, and dim, brownish daylight filtered into the room. A single bed was placed under one window with a wooden nightstand beside it and a chest of drawers. It was the most unpretentious room Leigh had ever seen. Precisely what she needed.

She crossed to one of the windows and folded back the shutters to let in the daylight. She opened the window and a gust of perfumed air wafted into the room. A blossom spun down from the plumeria tree and landed on the windowsill. Leigh picked it up and sniffed it.

''That's a sign of good luck,'' George said behind her. Leigh turned. He set her suitcase and tote bag on the floor near the door. "You know, like the Chinese with their butterflies."

Leigh laughed. "Seems appropriate, doesn't it? You know, George, I'm going to like it here."

"I sure hope so. It's a simple life but a happy one, I guess—if you like the simple life."

Leigh heard the note of doubt in his voice, but did not comment on it. She turned to look out the window. "At the moment I'm starved for a little simplicity. You're looking at a burned-out city girl." She peered through the stand of trees beyond the bungalow. "I can't see Simon's house from here," she said. "The trees are blocking the view."

"The people who built this place planned it that way," George said. "This was the caretaker's cottage. The family in the big house wanted their privacy."

"Simon doesn't have a caretaker anymore?"

"It's just that none of his help lives in. We all live nearby and come to work in the morning. So he's been using this place for storage until now. He even had the phone taken out, so you'll have to make your calls from his house." George looked around to see if he had missed anything. "Well, I guess I'll be going. If you need anything, just tell Simon. He'll be down to see you later. Aloha." He flashed a smile and left.

Florence was in her room, sitting on the bed. She looked up at Leigh as she drew off her shoes. "I think I'm going to lie down for a while, if you don't mind. Airline flights always wear me out."

"I don't mind at all. I'm going to change and go down to the beach." Leigh started for her room and then stopped and turned back. She pulled out the olivine pendant from inside her blouse. "Can I ask just one question? Where did you get this?"

"Hmm?" Florence looked at the pendant, which turned slowly back and forth as Leigh held it by the chain. Florence frowned. "Let's see. . . . Wasn't that in my jewelry chest?"

Leigh tried to rein in her impatience. Florence's vague moments were quite frustrating and a little premature. She was only fifty. "Yes, but you gave it to me. You said you got it the first time you came to Hawaii."

"I did? I suppose that's where I got it, then."

"But *where?*"

"Oh, heavens, I don't remember. That was almost thirty years ago. I don't even remember that trip."

"On the back it says *Souza—Oahu.* Look. See that?"

"Well, then, I'm sure I picked it up in some little shop in Waikiki. I can't imagine why. It isn't a very pretty thing, is it?" She lay back on the bed and closed her eyes.

Leigh sighed. She knew better than to pursue the conversation any further. Aunt Florence had always been vague about certain things; she refused to work her brain over whatever did'nt interest her.

Leigh went into her room and changed into her bathing suit. She took off the olivine pendant and looked at it. What was it about this ugly little rock that had made Malcolm react so strongly? Maybe it had some hidden meaning that only islanders were aware of. Or maybe Malcolm was just a very weird person. Leigh was glad she wouldn't see him again.

She tucked the pendant into the lid of her suitcase. She would think of a more appropriate place to put it later. At the moment she was in a hurry to get down to the beach.

The hot sun soaked deliciously into Leigh's skin as she lay stretched out on her beach towel on the black-sand beach below the bungalow. Her eyes were closed; she listened to the roar and sigh of the waves as they rushed up on the shore and ebbed away. The salty ocean scent mingled with the smell of warm coconut oil in the suntan lotion she had smoothed over her body. Leigh smiled and snuggled her back into the beach towel. In Hawaii only a couple of hours, she had already attained bliss.

She had the odd exhilaration of time standing still. For as long as she could remember, her life had been a blur. She had been salutatorian of her high-school class, then had gone on to major in pre-law at UCLA. She had never let the grass grow under her feet, as her father had often said of her with great pride. She was a lot like her father, who was vice-president in charge of imports for a large electronics firm in Los Angeles. Both of them were ambitious and charming and single-minded. No, they never let the grass grow under their feet.

At five feet eight, Leigh had been urged by more than one person during her college years to go into modeling. She had blue-green eyes, perfect teeth, and glossy light-brown hair that fell to her waist. But she wanted to do more with her life than be a Barbie doll for designers to dress up. She had been very happy when, a month after being accepted at law school, she had landed a position as a paralegal at Townsend & Kohler, one of the most respected law firms in the city.

But after four years of juggling law school with her work at Townsend & Kohler, the pace of her life was starting to get to her. She had had a couple of relationships since college, one with a sweet young man who needed to be led around by the nose, and the other more recently, with a suave lawyer who took himself and his degree from Harvard Law School quite seriously and who treated Leigh like his subordinate. She had ended that relationship at a dinner party in front of his amazed colleagues.

It was then that she knew she needed to get away from the world of law, needed to reexamine what it was she truly wanted out of life. So when Aunt Florence asked her to go to Hawaii with her to visit an old friend, Leigh had accepted. The fact that the old friend was a retired attorney had not been enough to dissuade her from a much-needed vacation.

So here she was, lying on a beach in Hawaii, glad to be away from the pressures of her job, glad to be rid of the latest man in her life. And yet she felt a void. It was an emptiness she had carried around for years, though until recently she had been too busy to notice. Perhaps, after all, that was the motivation behind the flurry in her life—so she wouldn't miss what she needed most and had tried without success to find: a man strong enough to stand on his own, kind enough to support her when she was down, confident enough to turn to her for help when he needed it. Such a man was hard to find. It was even harder to find one who took her breath away, yet she would settle for nothing less.

Not many people understood how she felt, least of all her mother, who had been terribly disappointed when Leigh failed to bag that eminently eligible young attorney. She could not explain to her mother, to whom the joys of domestic life meant a great deal, that the single life was far preferable to being married to the wrong man.

Leigh opened her eyes and sat up. The sun beating against her closed eyelids had washed the color from her sight and for a moment her world was black and white. Slowly the color returned to the scene before her. She shaded her eyes with her hand and looked out at the sea. Waves broke against the shore and slid up onto the black sand. Further out, tumbled rocks jutted out of the sapphire water. She could hear George's warning about the lava rocks in her head.

As if in challenge to his warning, a figure appeared on the beach a few hundred yards away and waded into the water with long, sure strides. He was a tall young man with wavy black hair and sun-bronzed skin. He dove under the water with a confidence that could only come with familiarity. Leigh drew in her breath but then relaxed. He must know what he was doing. He probably lived nearby, in one of the houses she had seen farther down the shore. But as the minutes passed and he did not surface, Leigh grew worried. She suddenly sprang to her feet, concerned for his safety.

He surfaced, abruptly, a long way from where he had gone under, water streaming from his hair and muscular shoulders. With powerful strokes he swam out past a mass of rocks and disappeared.

She smiled at herself. She could hardly swim the length of an Olympic-size pool, yet until a moment ago she had been preparing to save the life of someone who could probably swim from here to Maui.

She decided to take a walk. Behind her, two paths disappeared into a fringe of palm trees. One led back to the bungalow. She would find out where the other one went. She slipped into her terry-cloth robe and her beach sandals and started off on the long walk that eventually led her to a small family plot.

He stood between the trunks of two trees, watching her. Leigh's heart, pounding wildly, slowed to a more regular rhythm when she saw that he was not Malcolm but the tall young man she had seen swimming earlier.

Looking at him now, as he stood a mere six feet away from her, Leigh was reminded of the *ali'i,* the ancient Hawaiian royalty she had read about. He was at least six feet two, broad-chested, and broad-shouldered. He wore a brown tank top that matched the color of his skin. His wavy black hair, still damp from his swim, hung just long enough to brush the back of his neck.

"I'm really sorry," Leigh said. "I know I have no business here. It's just that the tombstones looked so—fascinating, I'm sorry."

"Gravestones are meant to be read. You've done nothing wrong."

Leigh looked up, surprised. He smiled. His dark eyes

were wide and gentle. "You're new here," he said. "I haven't seen you before."

"My aunt and I are here on vacation from California."

"Welcome to Hawaii. My name is Kalani Akina."

"It's a pleasure to meet you. I'm Leigh Christie." She held out her hand, the perfect professional, before she realized how out of place the gesture was. She caught him by surprise, but he smiled and put out his large, long-fingered hand in hers. His grip around her hand was firm yet almost a caress. Something electric leaped up Leigh's arm. She was glad to see that he wore no rings of any kind. Allowing her hand to rest in his a moment too long, she finally extricated it and bent to retrieve her beach bag.

"Will this path take me back around to the road?"

"Yes. Would you like me to show you? I'm headed that way anyway. I'm going to help my father close up the store."

"The store." Suddenly Leigh made the connection. "Oh, Akina! Akina's General Store! We passed it on the road coming here. You must do a great business. It's the only store I saw after we left Hilo."

"We do a good business."

They came out of the tunnel of trees into the bright sunlight. "I saw you swimming earlier," she said. "I was sitting on the beach. You're a good swimmer."

"It comes naturally, living here. I'm an assistant swim coach at the University at Hilo, and that helps too."

"I guess it would! Are you off for the summer?"

"Yes. I came back home to help my father with his

business. But that's just an excuse, really. Since I got my own place in Hilo, I miss this valley. I come back whenever I can.''

Leigh watched him as he spoke. In spite of his casual clothes, he carried himself regally. She found herself wanting to walk close to him, wanting to reach up and touch the rich skin and smooth planes of his face. He glanced down at her then and must have caught something in her expression, for he gave her a slow, quiet smile that made her heart leap. She glanced away quickly. It was unlike her to give herself away so soon.

They reached the road and Leigh turned to the right when she saw the sign leading to Wailani. Kalani continued on to the left.

"Here, down this way," Leigh said. "We're staying at Wailani."

Kalani stopped and turned. He glanced at the sign and then at her. All benevolence drained from his face. "Wailani?"

"Yes."

"Is Simon Trowbridge a friend of yours?"

"He and my aunt have been friends for years. You know him?"

A wry smile curved his lips. "Yeah. I know him."

"Well, when I see him, I'll tell him I ran into you—"

"It probably would be better if you didn't."

Leigh was startled into silence.

Kalani nodded past her down the road. "Can you find your way from here? I really should be getting to the store."

"Oh, sure. Thank you for bringing me this far."

He smiled politely and turned away.

Leigh watched him go, a Hawaiian prince, his dark head aglow in the afternoon sunlight, away from her and Wailani and Simon Trowbridge.

## Chapter Two

Leigh returned to the bungalow and climbed the wooden stairs, letting her beach bag bang tiredly against each step. At the top of the stairs she stopped.

Florence sat in one of the chairs at the far end of the veranda. In the other chair sat a striking, long-legged man who looked to be in his mid-fifties. They both turned to look at Leigh and the man immediately rose out of his chair. He was quite tall.

"There you are, Leigh!" Florence said brightly as she got up. "I was wondering when you were going to be back. I want you to meet my dear friend and our host, Simon Trowbridge. Simon, this is my niece, Leigh Christie. She's about to graduate from law school and is currently a paralegal with Townsend & Kohler in Los Angeles."

Leigh crossed the veranda and held out her hand to him. "No one could accuse my aunt of making dry introductions. It's very nice to meet you, Simon."

His long-fingered hand took hers in a warm grip. "Let me make the rather unprofessional observation that you are probably driving every male attorney at

18

Townsend & Kohler crazy. You have the loveliest eyes and hair I have ever seen." His deep-set hazel eyes turned to Florence. "The eyes are a family trait, I see." He squeezed Leigh's hand and released it.

She smiled. Smooth. He was a charmer, no doubt about it, which explained why he had been so successful in his law practice. Through her smile Leigh studied him, wondering why exactly it was best that she not mention Kalani Akina to him. It was not unusual for lawyers to have enemies. It was a hazard of the profession. Yet Leigh was curious how the elegant gentleman before her had alienated the Hawaiian prince she had met this afternoon.

"Did you have a nice swim?" Simon continued.

"Yes, it was great. Thank you for having us here. We're really going to enjoy the next four weeks."

"You're more than welcome. I'm sure you'll have dozens of friends by the time you leave. By the way, I'm sorry I wasn't there to meet you at the airport. There was some plantation business that just couldn't wait."

"Oh, Simon, you don't need to apologize about that," Florence said. "I can imagine that a sugar plantation is a full-time job. Even though you *are* supposed to be retired."

"Only from my law practice. Never from Wailani."

"Tell Leigh about all the hiring you're doing now," Florence said.

"Well," Simon began as he seated himself on the veranda railing, "harvest is less than six weeks away, and I need a lot of workers. Fortunately, there are always plenty of high school and college kids around during the summer. In the next few weeks they'll be swarming to all the plantation offices on the island to sign up. As soon as we've burned the fields, we can put them to work.''

"As soon as you've burned the fields?'' Florence asked. "Why on earth would you do that?''

"Sounds ridiculous, doesn't it? Actually, it's a trick of the trade that was discovered quite by accident around the turn of the century. Rats have always been a problem in Hawaii, especially in the cane fields. They became such a plague for one planter that he decided to sacrifice his crop to get rid of them. So he set his whole field on fire. Sure enough, he got rid of the rats, and all the foliage—but the canes were left standing. He decided to go through and see if the crop was salvageable. When he tried one of the canes, he discovered it was the sweetest thing he'd ever tasted. Not only had the fire gotten rid of the rats, it had cured his sugarcane! It wasn't long before word got around and the practice caught on. Now it's standard procedure.''

"I wish I could do that to my room,'' Leigh said. "Set fire to it once a week to get rid of the junk and leave the good stuff standing.''

"Oh, honestly, Leigh!'' Florence exclaimed. "Wouldn't it be easier to use your drawers and your wastebasket? From the looks of your room I'm sure that's never occurred to you.''

Leigh grinned.

"Mistah Trowbridge? Mistah Trowbridge!''

Simon looked over his shoulder at someone standing below the veranda. Leigh went to the railing and looked down. An old Hawaiian woman was standing by the stairs, her body cocked to one side to accommodate the weight of the burlap bag slung over her shoulder. Her thin, graying hair was pulled up into a tight knot on top of her head; she wore a faded red floral muumuu and rubber zoris.

"Good afternoon, Emma," Simon said. "What can I do for you?"

"I jus' went to your house to get the laundry," Emma said, in a strong pidgin accent. "Derek told me you want Ko'a to work tonight. That right?"

"That's right."

"How come? It's her day off."

"Yes, but I have special guests this evening and I'd like her to help with dinner. I already spoke with her. She said she'd be glad to."

"Chee! All right. Long as she say so." Emma's gaze shifted to Leigh. "This your guest?"

"Yes, she and her aunt are visiting from California." At this Florence went to the railing on the other side of Simon. "Florence, this is Emma Luahine, one of the local women."

Florence smiled graciously at the woman. "How do you do?"

Emma looked up at Florence and Leigh. She heaved the burlap bag to the other shoulder, glanced oddly at Simon, and then turned and headed toward the drive. She crossed to the beach path and disappeared from sight.

"Interesting woman," Florence said carefully.

"Once you get to know Emma, you'll find out that her bark is worse than her bite. Her granddaughter works for me part-time, and she's a love. She's the light of Emma's life. Coral's parents died when she was a baby and Emma raised her. They're pretty close.'' Simon looked at his watch. ''Well. I'd better let you ladies get ready for dinner. I'll have George pick you up about seven and bring you up to the house.''

''Oh, Simon, don't bother that poor young man,'' Florence protested. ''Heavens, if we can't walk up a little hill I don't know what.''

''It's a dirt drive and it's farther than you think. Please. Indulge me.''

''Silliest thing I ever heard. . . .''

Simon smiled. ''See you at dinner.'' He crossed the veranda to the stairs and turned and waved to them. Leigh saw the soft smile on her aunt's lips and said nothing.

Aunt Florence was an elegant widow. Twenty-three years ago, at the age of twenty-seven, the lovely, charming Florence Christie had married a successful attorney, Ross Barclay, and joined the upper echelons of San Francisco society. It was a position to which she was well-suited, for Florence knew how to be a gracious hostess, a delightful dinner companion, and an unerring social secretary.

She and Ross never had children. It was the only part of her life she would have changed; and, to fill that gap, she became a sort of fairy godmother to Leigh, her brother's only child. As Leigh was growing up, Aunt Florence had always meant presents and expensive restaurants and concert tickets. Such lavish generosity made it easier for Leigh to overlook Florence's vague moments, when she didn't seem to know where or even who she was. The moments were brief, and, because Leigh could not remember a time when Florence had not had them, she accepted them as part of her aunt's otherwise charming personality.

Uncle Ross had died five years ago, and since then Aunt Florence had done a great deal of traveling. She had, of course, been to Hawaii several times before—but this was her first visit to Simon Trowbridge's estate.

"Leigh, do these shoes go with this dress? Tell me honestly," Florence said.

"Yes, they do. It looks like you bought them to wear together."

"I did, but I just want to be sure. And what about the scarf? Too much?"

"No, the scarf looks nice. You look great. And we're going to be late for dinner if you don't hurry."

"I'm almost ready. You look very nice, I must say. That blue-green dress matches your eyes, and I love the shirred sleeves. All right, let's go."

They left the bungalow and started up the drive toward Simon's home. The sun sat on the crest of the Kohala mountain range to the west; to the east, the ocean glowed from pink to slate-blue as it lost the last rays of daylight.

As they headed up the drive, Leigh became aware of faraway voices and occasional plinks from a guitar. She stopped and turned. The sounds wafted up from the beach. Leigh went to the edge of the road and peered down.

In the midst of the palm grove she could see the flicker of a bonfire. Small groups of people sat on the sand around it and listened to an unseen guitar player. Soon a percussion player joined him. Someone started to sing.

Leigh stared down at the scene. How she would love to spend twilight on a Hawaiian beach, warm sand underneath her, music in her ears, a tall Hawaiian prince nearby. . . .

She jerked herself back to reality and hurried to catch up with her aunt.

The drive wound slowly up a gentle hill, lined on either side with bamboo and ferns. As they rounded the curve they saw the welcoming lights of Simon's house. A moment later they heard an engine behind them. Leigh looked over her shoulder. Two headlights flashed and bounced up the drive toward them. As they got closer, Leigh saw it was George's Jeep.

He braked to a halt beside them and gave them a white-toothed smile. "Get in, ladies! Why are you walking when Simon told you I would pick you up?"

"We told him not to bother," Florence said, but she looked truly relieved as she climbed into the Jeep. Her high-heel pumps had not been made with hiking in mind.

Leigh climbed into the back and they took off up the hill, bouncing and careening with the wind in their faces. Florence literally hung onto her hat. By the time they screeched to a halt in front of Simon's front gate, Leigh was breathless and exhilarated.

She climbed out of the Jeep and helped Florence out. The older woman stopped in front of a bamboo gate, straightened her clothes and smoothed her hair, and gave George a tight-lipped smile.

"Thank you for the ride," she said.

George flicked a salute from an arched eyebrow. "Sure. Just go on in through the gate to the front door. See you later." He smiled at Leigh and put the Jeep in first gear. With a crunch and splatter of gravel, he executed a U-turn and bounced off down the drive.

Leigh watched him go with a twinge of envy. He was probably on his way to that bonfire on the beach.

The bamboo gate opened into an enclosed courtyard. Leigh and Florence went in, closing the gate behind them. The stone walkway that led to the front door was lit by a series of pagoda lights; to the right, a floodlit fountain trickled and splashed in a basin of black lava rock.

Florence rang the doorbell and gave a last pat to her hair. The door was promptly opened by a young Hawaiian man dressed in a white gauze shirt, white pants, and zoris.

"Aloha. Please come in. Mr. Trowbridge is waiting in the living room—"

"No, I just couldn't wait," Simon said as he approached from behind the houseboy. "Florence, you lovely thing! I'm going to have my friends over soon so I can show you off. And you look ravishing, Leigh." He embraced them both and turned to the houseboy. "Thank you, Derek. Please see to dinner."

Simon led them into the living room, where they sat down on a pastel-print sofa while he walked over to the wet bar in the corner. The far wall was enclosed by ceiling-to-floor picture windows that framed a magnificent view of the ocean and, off to the left, an occasional flash of light.

"What's that?" Leigh asked.

"The lighthouse at Point Maka'u. It's at the far end of the valley."

"A lighthouse? Oh, I'd love to see it!"

"Don't expect too much. It's nothing like those picturesque lighthouses in New England. This one is just a flashing strobe light on top of a steel mesh tower. Totally automated. Someone goes out there once a month to maintain it."

"How disappointing," Leigh commented.

Simon smiled. "Don't worry. Our island will make it up to you. Florence? Do you still drink Bloody Marys?"

"Oh, yes."

"How about you, Leigh?"

"I'll have a screwdriver, please."

"Sure. Dinner is about ready, so I'll make our drinks and we'll go in." He mixed the drinks and poured himself a scotch, then escorted them to the airy dining room. They sat down and Derek began to serve a delicious meal of baked ham with pineapple, rice, and various salads.

"Your house is beautiful," Leigh said. "Have you always lived in Hawaii?"

Simon took a sip of his scotch and shook his head. "I was born in Detroit, believe it or not. The first time I laid eyes on Hawaii was over fifty years ago. I had just turned eighteen and joined the Navy, and they stationed me at Pearl Harbor. I fell in love with Hawaii. After my Navy stint I managed to get into the University of Hawaii, and I've been here ever since—

except for the three years I was away at law school, of course.''

While he spoke, Leigh studied him. Simon's dark-brown hair was feathered with white at the temples, and the backs of his hands were veined with blue; otherwise he showed little signs of age. Yet if he had been eighteen over fifty years ago, he must be near seventy.

After dinner they returned to the spacious living room. It was more subtly lit now, with the soft upward wash of light from two torchière lamps that stood on either side of the sofa. Derek brought in a blue china coffeepot and matching cups and saucers on a tray, which he set on the low glass table in front of the sofa, and left the room.

Simon took up the coffeepot. ''Coffee, Florence? It's Kona's best.''

''Yes, please. Cream and sugar, if you have it.''

''Of course. Leigh? Do you drink coffee?''

''No, thanks. But I'll take a Pepsi if you've got one.''

Simon prepared Florence's coffee and handed her the cup on a saucer. She took it and wandered toward the picture windows.

''Do you mind if I admire your view?''

''I'd be disappointed if you didn't.'' Simon passed Leigh her glass of Pepsi. ''Why don't we go outside? It's a pleasant evening.'' He pulled open a sliding glass door and gestured them out onto the flagstone patio.

The twilight sky was deep blue, dotted with tiny diamond stars; a lingering glow hovered over Wailani and the bay below.

Simon held Florence's elbow and gestured as he talked; she nodded and sipped her coffee. With Leigh walking just behind, he led them slowly around the house to a terrace overlooking a small, grassy vale dominated by an immense banyan tree; beyond the vale the darkened cliffs of Honola'i rose above the tree line.

"You can't see them now, but at the far side of that vale below us, on the other side of the banyan, are the stables. You're welcome to go riding any time you like. Do you enjoy riding?" he asked Leigh.

"A lot." She went to the edge of the flagstone terrace and peered down into the dusky vale. The stables eluded her sight. All that was visible were a dozen or so ghostly pale rectangular shapes.

Leigh narrowed her eyes. She strained forward, trying to make out the shapes. "Are those tombstones?" she asked, pointing.

Simon and Florence stopped talking. Leigh looked up at them. With an uneasy glance down the hill, Simon guided Florence away from the edge of the terrace. "Yes. That's the York family plot. The York family built this place around the turn of the century and they buried their dead down there. Phoebe York Hampton, the last of the line, is buried there. Now, if you'd both like to come this way, I'll show you the gazebo at the back of the house. It has a spectacular view of Honola'i Valley."

Simon and Florence moved off in the dusk as the lights of Wailani came on. Leigh watched them go. Simon's uneasiness about the York family burial plot bothered her. She glanced down into the vale. The tombstones were no longer visible.

She rose to her feet and turned back to the house, holding her now-empty Pepsi glass. She went inside and headed toward the kitchen.

Pushing open the swinging door, she saw the kitchen was immense. It had obviously been built with dozens of guests in mind. Renovations had been made over the years; a coffeemaker and microwave oven were built in under the counter along with a dishwasher. A young woman in a black uniform and white apron loaded dishes into it while Derek watched her, his elbows on the counter and his chin in his hands. Leigh could see at a glance that he was hopelessly in love.

"I got the car fixed, Coral," he was saying. "Maybe next week I'll give you a ride to the party, yeah?"

"Oh, you got your car fixed! Good. I know it's been giving you trouble for a long time."

"Yeah, but—"

"Derek, please bring over that stack of dishes for me."

Leigh cleared her throat. Derek and Coral looked around.

Leigh could see why Derek was so taken. Coral had soft, luminous dark eyes and a sweet smile. Her curly black hair was caught up in a bun at the nape of her neck, but a few wisps had escaped and curled charmingly around her face.

"Hi," Leigh said, as she crossed the kitchen toward them. "I don't know if I'm supposed to be here, but my mother always taught me to take my dirty dishes to the sink." She smiled rather lamely and held out her empty Pepsi glass.

Coral took the glass and smiled. "You didn't have to do that. But thank you."

"My name is Leigh. I met your grandmother this afternoon. She came to the bungalow while Simon was there."

"I hope the bungalow is comfortable. It hasn't been used for anything but storage in a long time."

"Oh, we love it. It's a cute little place."

Coral nodded and said nothing.

Leigh glanced at Derek. His arms were folded across his chest and he looked put out. *I'm stealing his time with Coral,* Leigh thought. "Well, I'd better go before they wonder what happened to me." She gave Coral a friendly smile and pushed open the swinging door.

Florence and Simon still had not returned to the living room. Leigh clasped her hands behind her back and strolled idly around the room, studying the pictures and objects that decorated it.

Twin bookcases lining the wall were filled with legal texts. Leigh blithely ignored them. She was just starting to get the knots out of her psyche and did not want to be reminded of work.

Between the bookcases was a drop-leaf desk. It was stacked with law books, stationery, a brass letter opener, a pencil sharpener. Leigh sat down in the swivel chair, grabbed the underside of the desk, and pulled herself toward it. As she did the center drawer came open. Leigh started to push it shut. Then she saw the gun.

It lay casually in the front corner of the drawer. It was a revolver, and looked like a prop in a movie. But

Leigh knew it was real. Why did Simon have a gun in his desk?

She pushed the drawer closed. The desk rocked slightly and something tumbled off one of the shelves. Leigh picked it up. It was a photograph in a silver frame of a young woman who stood in front of a sign that read *University of Hawaii* and smiled at the camera. She wore a dark-green sleeveless sheath dress and black high heels. Her smooth dark hair curved just under her jawline. She looked about twenty.

A large hand pulled the picture out of Leigh's grasp. Her head snapped up. Simon opened the desk drawer and slid the photograph inside. In the same motion he picked up the gun. Leigh gasped.

"Look at this, Florence," he said. It was then Leigh noticed her aunt behind him. She had not heard their return.

"What, Simon?" Florence asked. Leigh realized she hadn't seen the picture.

"This revolver. Navy issue. I've had this baby almost fifty years." He spun the cylinder.

Florence came over and looked at the gun. "Aren't you afraid to keep that thing in the house?"

"No. It isn't loaded. I have a box of cartridges here in the drawer, but I never load it unless I'm going to take it out for target practice."

"Well, I wouldn't want one of those things in my house—loaded or unloaded."

Simon smiled and returned the revolver to the drawer. He closed it with a snap and walked away without a word to Leigh.

Later, Simon drove Leigh and Florence back to the

bungalow in his Mercedes. He parked in front of the steps and walked them up to the door. The night air was warm and heavy.

"It's been a delightful evening, ladies," he said. "The first of many, I hope. Florence, I intend to give a party in your honor so you can meet all my friends."

"Oh, Simon, how lovely!"

"I've taken the liberty of sending out the invitations. It'll be a week from Wednesday."

"That'll be perfect."

"But, Aunt Florence—" Leigh began. Simon and Florence both turned to look at her as if they had forgotten she was there. She felt like a fly in the ointment. "Don't you remember? We're going to be in Honolulu a week from Wednesday."

There was a silence. Florence bit her lip. "Oh, that's right. That'll be in the middle of our week there, won't it?"

"Why don't you shorten your stay?" Simon suggested. "You can usually see most of the high points of Honolulu in three or four days."

Florence immediately brightened. "Why, that's a wonderful idea! Leigh, dear, would you mind awfully? Thank you, you're sweet. Simon, may I call the airline from your place tomorrow morning?"

"Of course. Leigh, I hope this doesn't put too much of a kink in your plans, but I promise you this will be a party to be remembered." He lifted Florence's hand to his lips and kissed it. "I'll see you tomorrow." He gave Leigh an unreadable look and left.

\*    \*    \*

It was still dark when Leigh awoke with a start. For a moment she did not know where she was. She sat up in bed and looked around the tiny bedroom. Immediately it all came back to her. She was in Hawaii with Aunt Florence, in Simon Trowbridge's bungalow.

She drew up her legs and wrapped her arms around them. How strange to be awake now. She was a sound sleeper and usually did not stir until the morning sun beat through her window. She wondered what had awakened her.

A warm, moist breeze wafted in through the partly open window behind her. She turned and breathed in the scent of plumeria. Above the treetops a half moon hung in the sky, obscured now and then by the clouds scudding past its face.

When Leigh heard the noise she knew immediately she had heard it before—it had awakened her. A muffled cry, a creak, a sob. Leigh froze, straining to determine where the sounds had come from.

The voice came again. It was Aunt Florence. Leigh sprang out of bed and ran to her aunt's room. Florence tossed and turned in her bed, which creaked with every movement. "Where is he?" she muttered.

"Where is who?" Leigh asked before she realized her aunt was asleep. She went to her bedside and put her hand on her aunt's shoulder. "Aunt Florence?"

She sat straight up in bed. "The crouching lion! The crouching lion!"

Leigh stumbled backward, nearly choking with fright. She caught herself and went toward the bed again.

"Elizabeth?" Florence cried. "Elizabeth, where are you?"

Elizabeth. That was Leigh's middle name. After her grandmother, Florence's mother.

Leigh grabbed Florence's shoulders. "Wake up! You're having a nightmare!"

Florence slumped back against the pillow. Leigh felt a tear fall on the back of her hand. "I can't find him. I can't."

Leigh peered at her aunt in the dark. In spite of the warm night she felt a chill steal over her. She shook her shoulders again. "Aunt Florence?"

"What is it, dear?"

Leigh looked closer at Florence's face. Her eyes were open. "Are—are you awake?"

"Why, yes." Florence sat up in bed and flicked on the small bedside lamp. "What's wrong, Leigh? You look as if you'd seen a ghost."

She gulped. "Aunt Florence, you were having a nightmare! Don't you remember? You were screaming about some lion that was ready to jump on you."

Florence looked blank.

"You don't remember the dream? Apparently the lion had already gotten one of your friends, because you said you couldn't find him."

Florence started to laugh. "Did I really say all those things? How silly."

"Well, I'm glad you think it's funny. You scared the living daylights out of me."

"I'm sorry. But I'm fine, really. Go back to bed now, Leigh."

"All right. But no more nightmares, okay?"

"Okay. Good night." Florence smiled and snapped off the lamp.

Leigh made her way back to her own room. As she climbed back into bed she glanced out the window at the cloud-veiled moon. A movement caught her eye. She dropped her gaze. A man was standing among the trees in front of the bungalow.

Leigh's heart began to thud. Slowly, on weak legs, she crept to the window.

He was still there, partly obscured by the low-hanging branch of a tree. Leigh could not see his face. At that moment he must have seen her at the window, for he turned and disappeared from view.

Leigh watched for a long time, but he did not return. Finally, in spite of the warm night, she secured the shutters and closed the window. She climbed back into bed and burrowed down under the covers.

## Chapter Three

The next morning, Leigh said nothing to Florence about the watcher outside the window. After breakfast George arrived in his Jeep to take them up to Simon's house.

"Simon wants me to come for you every morning unless he comes himself," George told them as they drove up the hill.

"That's very nice, but we never meant to turn you into a shuttle service," Florence said.

"I don't mind. It only takes a few minutes, and from here I go straight to the plantation office."

They pulled up in front of Simon's gate and Florence climbed out of the Jeep. "Thank you again, George."

Leigh turned to George. "Listen, can I come with you? I'll walk back from the plantation office. I want to explore a little."

"Sure! It's a long walk back, though. You really want to do it?"

"I'm sure. I'd rather go for a long walk than sit indoors on a morning like this." She turned to Florence. "You understand, don't you?"

"Of course. I'm sure the pace that Simon and I keep

is much slower than you're used to. But we can expect you for lunch, can't we?''

"Yes. I'll be back in a couple of hours.''

Florence wiggled her fingers in farewell and opened the gate into Simon's courtyard. George turned the Jeep around and he and Leigh headed back down the hill.

"I'm glad I'm going with you this time,'' Leigh said as Simon's house disappeared behind them. "I was so jealous last night when you dropped us off and drove away.''

"Really? Why?''

"Because I was sure you were headed for that bonfire I saw down on the beach.''

He grinned with an appreciative lift of his eyebrows. "You're pretty smart. Yeah, that's where I went. There's going to be another one tonight. Do you want to—''

"I'd love to.''

He grinned. "Great! I can come for you about seven.''

"No, no,'' she said with a playful wag of her finger. "We don't want to turn you into a shuttle service. I can walk down myself. I'll see you there.''

He gave an easy shrug of his shoulders then glanced at her, smiling. "You always so independent?''

"Always. It used to drive my boyfriend crazy.''

"Until he got used to it?''

"Until we broke up.''

George gave a long whistle. "No guy's gonna break your stride, is he?''

At one time Leigh would have been pleased by such

a comment, but now she was not so sure it was something to be proud of.

They reached the main road and headed up into the valley. They continued into the heart of Honola'i, and houses and taro patches soon gave way to rolling acres of sugarcane. A low clapboard building appeared to the right of the road and George pulled off onto the red clay parking area in front. They came to a halt in a cloud of red dust.

"Here we are. I'd better get inside. My dad took the workers out to the field in the truck three hours ago. I'm sure he left me a lot of paperwork."

"Thanks for the ride, George," Leigh said as she climbed out of the Jeep. "I'll just follow the road back toward Wailani. I'm sure I'll find some interesting things along the way."

"See you tonight down on the beach."

She nodded and waved and turned toward the road. Sunlight warmed the red earth under her sandaled feet and a gentle breeze rustled the sugarcane on both sides of the road. The satisfying smell of rich soil came up to her as she trudged back down the road.

With each step she grew more aware of how far she had to go. She had not realized how deep into the valley the plantation office was. She would do well if she made it back to Wailani by noon—if she did nothing but walk.

After she had gone about a quarter of a mile, the wall of sugarcane on the left side of the road suddenly opened up to reveal a service road cutting through the cane field. Leigh stopped. She could not see Wailani from here, but she remembered that it lay roughly ahead and to the left. If she cut through the cane field, she was sure she could lop at least a mile off her walk.

She struck off down the red dirt service road. Sugarcane rose up over her head on either side. The plantation office had disappeared. The morning grew strangely silent.

Leigh quickened her steps, trying to shake off the eerie feeling that followed her. She heard scuttling amongst the sugarcane. *Rats,* she thought. Simon had said they were a problem. *Hurry, hurry.*

Another service road intersected the first. It seemed to lead directly toward Wailani so she took it still deeper into the cane field. Her heart began to thud as she thought of being lost in the sugarcane with only rats for company.

It was then that she heard another sound, so faint and faraway that at first she thought the steady beat-beat-beat was her heart in her ears. But the beating grew louder, accompanied by a low, mechanical hum. Leigh looked up and saw a helicopter headed toward her, flying unusually low over the cane fields.

She suddenly panicked and, heedless of the rats, hurried in among the sugarcane to avoid being hit. She crouched down to wait until the helicopter flew past. But when it reached her, it hovered for a moment and then swung slowly in a circle, barely twenty feet above her head. The wind of its propeller beat the sugarcane flat around her and whipped her hair wildly about her head. She stared up, terrified. The pilot had a pair of binoculars trained on her. She felt like a bug on a microscope slide. He lowered the binoculars and she saw his face clearly.

Malcolm.

The helicopter lifted and whirled away. Leigh sat in the midst of the sugarcane, breathless and frightened. The ensuing silence pressed in against her.

Abruptly, she thought of the watcher outside her window the night before. She knew it was Malcolm. He had found her and he was watching her. But why? What was so important about the ugly little pendant Aunt Florence had given her?

She stood up and began to run. She had to get out of the cane field. It seemed to go on and on forever, but at last she reached the road leading back to Wailani.

Leigh kept running. The red dust of the road sifted into her sandals and between her toes, but she hardly noticed. She felt that at any moment a helicopter might swoop down on her again. Even now she thought she heard the distant hum of a motor.

She did. Rather than a helicopter, however, a blue-and-gray Ford Bronco pulled up alongside her. She slowed her steps long enough to look at the driver. It was Kalani.

He leaned his head out the window. "Are you all right?"

Leigh stumbled to a stop. Fright and exertion had her heart pounding and her lungs ready to burst. For a moment she couldn't speak. Kalani climbed out of the car. A look of genuine concern was in his eyes as he came toward her. "What happened? Never mind, just get in the car. I'll give you a ride back."

Leigh allowed him to steer her around to the passenger side of the Bronco. He opened the door for her and she climbed in.

The back of the Bronco was packed with boxes and brown paper bags. Kalani climbed in behind the steering wheel and indicated his cargo with a jerk of his thumb over his shoulder.

"I'm on my way back from Kamuela. That's where we pick up most of the stock for my father's store. Besides, I'm having a party at my house this weekend and I needed a lot of supplies." He put the Bronco in gear and they took off down the road.

Leigh's breathing finally slowed to normal. "Thank you," she said. "I can't tell you how happy I am that you drove by at that particular moment."

"What happened?"

Leigh told him, and the story sounded strange even to her own ears. "I recognized the pilot," she said. "His name is Malcolm. I met him on the plane from Los Angeles and he frightened me even then."

Kalani said nothing, but his knuckles had gone white as he gripped the steering wheel. Leigh noticed the stony expression on his face. She sat back in her seat.

"You don't believe me, do you?"

He said nothing.

"Look, I didn't make it up. I don't have that active an imagination."

He looked at her. "I believe you, Leigh."

His words were small comfort. She could feel it again—that wall that had come down between them yesterday at the mention of Simon's name. For some reason, Kalani was treating her as an enemy.

He pulled off the road and came to a stop in front of the general store. "If you don't mind, I'll just take these boxes in to my father so he can stock the shelves. Then I'll drive you back to Wailani."

Leigh opened the door and climbed out. "Oh, no, don't bother. I'll be fine from here."

"But—"

"No, really. It's a short walk now. Thanks for the lift." Leigh shut the door and headed off down the road without looking back.

It seemed as if she and Kalani were destined to do nothing more than walk away from each other down a long red road.

It was five o'clock in the afternoon. The lowering sun bathed the landscape in its golden light. Leigh sat daydreaming in a chair on the veranda of the bungalow, her feet up on the railing, her toes almost touching the plumeria tree. A balmy breeze rustled through the tree and rippled her long hair. She closed her eyes and listened to the not-too-distant rush of the ocean.

A small, sharp twinge of yearning caught her unaware. *Come to me,* she thought. *Enfold me in your arms, let me feel your hand beneath my neck. I've been waiting for you so long. . . .*

She opened her eyes. Slowly, the feeling receded, until it was just a small flicker somewhere inside her.

The screen door banged. Leigh looked around. Florence crossed the veranda toward her, smiling.

"What are you doing, dear? Writing letters?"

Leigh glanced down at her lap. The letter she had started to write to her mother lay forgotten.

Florence sat down in the other chair. "It's a beautiful time of day, isn't it?" She looked off at the view with a complacent smile. "Simon has his own little paradise here. How sad that he has no family to share it with."

"Hasn't he ever been married?"

"Once. A long time ago. It didn't last very long."

Leigh thought of the silver-framed picture she had seen on his desk the evening before. "Did he love her?"

"I suppose he did. He doesn't like to talk about his past."

Leigh glanced at her aunt. Florence looked out at the view with narrowed eyes, as if she were thinking hard about something. Then she seemed to remember herself and glanced at Leigh. "Well. Have you any plans this evening?"

"Yes. I was invited to a bonfire down on the beach."

"A bonfire! Oh, dear. You won't set the island on fire, will you?"

"Aunt Florence—"

"Oh, I'm teasing. You go ahead, dear. Have fun!"

An hour later Leigh headed down the beach path, dressed in turquoise shorts and a white T-shirt. She had caught her hair into a loose ponytail with a turquoise clip, and it hung in a light-brown cascade over one shoulder.

She followed the gentle slope down to the beach. The sand was still warm, though the sun had slipped behind the Kohala Mountains. To her left the darkening ocean seemed to lie beneath transparent layers of color, gold and rose and blue. The waves whitened and broke into froth against the black rocks.

Up ahead she could see a fire beginning to flicker in a wide, shallow pit among the palm trees. Several dozen people sat around the fire on the sand. Among them Leigh recognized George and Coral.

A young man approached the group from the opposite direction with a guitar over his shoulder. He sat down and smiled and jerked his chin in greeting at several people. As Leigh drew closer she recognized him. It was Kalani.

She glanced away quickly, remembering her abrupt departure that morning. She glanced back. Her eyes met his. He smiled and gave her a tentative nod, as if he, too, were remembering how suddenly their meeting this morning had ended. Leigh smiled back. Their smiles met, melded, and created a new language that it seemed only the two of them could understand. *It's as if I've always known you,* Leigh thought. *Yet we've only just met.*

She heard George's voice calling her name. She looked toward him and waved to hide the fact that she resented his intrusion. He beckoned to her. "Come and sit down!"

Leigh entered the circle around the fire. "Hi, George. Hi, Coral," she said, and sat down on the sand beside the girl. To Leigh's left was Kalani. He had his ear to the guitar while he turned the tuning keys. She was intensely aware of his closeness.

A girl of about nineteen, with windblown dark hair, sauntered toward the bonfire, her hands shoved into the pockets of her billowing white pants. She wore a halter top of green-flowered cotton and scuffed her bare feet through the sand. When she spotted George, she made her way around the group toward him.

Leigh heard George draw a low sigh. But if it signified annoyance, he did not show it as he jerked his chin toward the girl in greeting.

"Hey, Debbie, how are you doing?"

Debbie came to a stop beside George. She looked Leigh over and did not respond to her smile. She sat down on George's other side.

"I come down to da fire, like everybody. Bother you?" she said.

"Eh, don't gimme dat stink-eye," George said, slipping easily into the local pidgin. "I just ask a friendly question."

"What you doing wit' dat girl? Is she your new chick?"

"Nah, she not. She come from L.A. fo' vacation." Then the pidgin was gone, "Leigh, this is Debbie Overgaard. Debbie, Leigh Christie."

"Hello," Leigh said pleasantly.

Debbie regarded her with sullen jealousy and turned back to George. Leigh looked at Coral, who shrugged and shook her head as if Debbie were not worth worrying about.

Leigh did not intend to. It was too lovely an evening. The sand was warm underneath her, and although the sun had set, the sky was still light. She watched the waves roll up onto shore and then slip away.

Then she saw something moving out on the water. Someone in a boat. It was an old woman, and she sat in the stern of the boat with her hand on the tiller of the outboard motor. Leigh recognized the stubborn set of her body. It was Emma. The boat sped by, bouncing over the water.

"There's your grandmother," Leigh said to Coral.

Coral nodded. "She's coming home from fishing. She stayed out a little too long. Now she's hurrying to get home before dark."

Leigh squinted her eyes. She watched the craft until it disappeared around a point of land. "She sure knows how to handle a boat."

"She's one of the best. And she makes sure everybody knows it too."

"Hey, Kalani," someone called. "Play us a song on that guitar!"

Kalani strummed a chord. "What do you want to hear?"

"One of your songs, man."

Kalani glanced at a young man who wore glasses and held a pair of bongos in his lap. "Hey, Raymond— you want to do 'Volcano'?"

Raymond adjusted the bongos on his lap. "Sure."

"All right," Kalani said, "this is a song Raymond wrote, and he's going to sing it. I'll harmonize." He struck two hard chords and started strumming to a driving beat supported by the bongos. Raymond began to sing.

*The ground it was a-shakin',*
*The sky it was a-smokin',*
*The tears were comin' to my eyes.*
*They called it Kilauea*
*But, brothah, I know bettah,*
*You better run before you die.*

And then Kalani joined in with the harmony.

*It ain't the lava that's gonna burn ya*
*It ain't the smoke that makes you cry.*
*The fire ain't comin' from deep in the ground*
*But from that pretty girl that's walkin' by.*

*She's a volcano*
*Don't look too long or you'll go blind.*
*She's a volcano*
*And, man, she'll drive you out of your mind.*
*She's gonna* getcha!

The last word was hissed rather than sung, and Kalani grinned as he continued strumming the guitar. Leigh watched him. His quiet facade concealed a deep inner fire that came out in his music. It was exciting to watch.

They went on to a second verse and finished the song with the same hissing "*getcha!*" The group around the fire laughed and clapped, then buzzed among themselves.

For a moment attention was drawn away from Kalani—all except Leigh's. She looked at him.

"You love it, don't you?" she asked quietly. "Your music."

His large brown hand stroked the polished body of the guitar. "It's food for my soul."

"Where do you find the time? I'm sure working at your father's store and at the university keeps you pretty busy."

"You make time for the things you love." His dark eyes caught the glint of the firelight and sent something soft and fiery through Leigh's heart.

"Listen," he continued, "I want to apologize for this morning. I was a little rude."

"No, you weren't," Leigh responded.

"Yes, I was. I told you I was having a party and didn't invite you to it. It's open invitation to everyone in the valley, but you couldn't have known that. Would you like to come?"

His voice was gentle and his eyes were kind. There did not seem to be a wall between them now. "Yes. Thank you."

"I live farther down the beach, beyond the boat ramp. You won't have any trouble finding the house."

Leigh smiled. Kalani glanced at her and then looked away. He strummed a few chords on his guitar.

Someone asked Kalani to play another song. For the moment Leigh had lost him. She turned toward Coral. But by now Derek had found his way to her side and was chatting eagerly. Coral smiled and nodded politely. Soon after, she quietly disappeared during one of Kalani's songs; Leigh turned and noticed she was gone.

Everyone else stayed on the beach until the fire was out and Kalani and Raymond covered the coals with sand. People said good night and started their separate ways toward home. George offered to walk Leigh back to the bungalow, but she firmly declined. She did not want to be seen alone with any man except one—and he had already left.

She headed up the beach alone. The night was dark and quiet. The ocean was a black void except for a green phosphorescence that glowed dimly at the crests of the waves.

The edge of a butter-colored moon appeared on the distant horizon and formed a wedge between black ocean and black sky. Slowly it emerged and shed a thin path of light across the water.

Leigh could see her way more clearly now. Coral's house came into view and Leigh walked past it toward the bungalow. She glanced up at Coral's porch, and stopped.

Coral sat on the veranda. The house behind her was dark, but the rising moon shone clearly on her face and on the person she was speaking to.

It was Malcolm.

## Chapter Four

Leigh was up early the next morning. She dressed in a white tank top and a pair of red cotton pants and went out to the small kitchen where Florence was boiling water for coffee. The bright morning sun slanted in through the kitchen window.

"You're up early," Florence said.

"Yes. It's amazing what fresh air and exercise can do." *And a head full of unsettling thoughts,* Leigh added silently to herself.

Florence opened the door of the refrigerator. She moved a few things around, her brow furrowed. "Oh, dear."

"What's the matter?"

"We're all out of eggs. And we're getting low on milk. I should have checked yesterday and said something to Simon." She regarded the interior of the refrigerator for a moment and then looked at Leigh. "Would you be a dear? I hate to bother Simon so early, and at any rate we shouldn't expect him to provide us with everything. I seem to remember a little general store about half a mile down the road. It shouldn't take

you long to walk down and pick up what we need. Do
you mind—?''

Akina's General Store. As far as Leigh knew, it was
the only store in Honola'i. ''No, I wouldn't mind. I'll
put on my sandals.''

Leigh followed the red dirt road that cut through the
green land and curved out of sight. A bright blue but-
terfly flitted past her. A soft breeze from the ocean
cooled her sun-soaked back. Leigh felt delicious. The
picture would have been perfect had it not been for the
one small, nagging thought in the back of her head.

She had seen Coral with Malcolm.

It was not a chance meeting—not at ten o'clock at
night on Coral's veranda. Who was Malcolm? And
what did Coral have to do with him?

The general store came into view, set off the road
in a spot cleared of the prolific vegetation. The pyra-
mid-shaped roof was thatched with palm fronds. The
walls were enclosed only about four feet up; above that
they were open except for the beams that supported
the roof. Bamboo awnings slanted out from these open
spaces, braced by sticks that could be removed to close
up the walls for the night.

Leigh went up the wooden steps and pulled open the
screen door. The man behind the front counter glanced
up and smiled at her.

There was no doubt that he was Kalani's father. He
was not as tall as Kalani, and his black hair was paint-
brush-straight whereas Kalani's had some wave. But
they shared the same broad shoulders, the same long,
dark, exotic eyes and high forehead. The smile, too,

was the same, though this man's came more readily than Kalani's. He must have been in his fifties, though there was not a line on his face nor a gray hair on his head.

Leigh found the eggs and milk and took them to the front counter. Kalani's father smiled as he rang up her purchases.

"Aloha," he said. "I haven't seen you before. Are you here on vacation?"

"Yes. My aunt and I are visiting Simon Trowbridge at Wailani." The man's smile faltered. Leigh remembered Kalani's similar reaction. "Are you Mr. Akina?"

His almond eyes crinkled. "Yes. And what's your name?"

"Leigh. I met Kalani the other day."

"Oh! Handsome boy, isn't he?"

"Yes. He looks a lot like you."

"You think Kalani looks like me? He has a lot of his mother in him—" He stopped abruptly. Leigh glanced at him. He smiled to cover over words he had not meant to say. "How long are you staying in Hawaii?"

"Four weeks."

"With Simon?"

"Most of the time. We're going to Honolulu for a few days next week."

"Of course. Everyone has to see Honolulu when they come to Hawaii." He reached under the counter for a paper bag, snapped it open, and put the milk and eggs inside.

Leigh heard footsteps on the porch. She glanced over

her shoulder. Kalani came into the store, lugging a large box that he set down with a thud just inside the door.

"What's that you brought?" Mr. Akina asked.

"The flour you ordered."

"What about the tea?"

"Ma's bringing it in." Kalani straightened up and started toward the counter. He paused when he saw Leigh.

She smiled. He did not return it, and she knew Simon's name still hung in the air between them. But again, behind the tension, she felt the words of their unspoken language, warm and caressing.

She picked up her small bag of groceries. "Hi. My aunt needed a couple of things."

"She's staying at Wailani." Mr. Akina said.

"I know," Kalani said.

Leigh gave them both a puzzled frown. "Well, thank you," she said, and turned toward the door.

She was met there by a tiny Asian woman carrying a small brown box. Kalani came to take it from her.

"I got it, Ma."

"Thanks, Kalani." She saw Leigh and nodded politely as she went into the store.

As Leigh started down the steps she glanced back through the screen door. Kalani and his father were both watching after her.

She walked back toward the bungalow. There were no houses along this stretch of road; most of the dwellings were set closer to the beach. Here there was only the tangled beauty of trees and vines and red-edged ti plants.

And something else. Leigh slowed her step, peering through the riot of greenery off the road. She spotted an angular shape that looked like the corner of a roof. It was overgrown with vines, concealed by trees. There was a small house back in there.

Curious, Leigh left the road to take a closer look. The place looked abandoned. The windows were all boarded up and the jungle had almost swallowed it up again.

When the door opened suddenly, she stifled a scream and darted behind a tree. A man came out of the house and closed the door. He looked around him, unaware of Leigh's presence.

It was Malcolm.

He descended the three steps that led to the house and headed toward her. She held her breath. He passed quite close without seeing her and disappeared through the trees.

She waited a long time until she was sure he was gone. Then she slipped out from behind the tree and hurried toward the house.

At the doorstep she stood still and listened. Absolute silence. No one else was in there. She set down the sack of groceries beside the door and tried the knob. The door creaked open.

The inside of the tiny house was very dark. Leigh stepped inside and waited for her eyes to adjust to the gloom. The room was crowded with large brown boxes with SUGAR stamped in black on their sides. Leigh knelt down and pulled open the flaps of the nearest box.

A powerful odor assaulted her nose. At first it smelled like a dead skunk. But then she recognized a strange sweetness that was not unfamiliar. She had smelled a diluted version of it wafting out of rest rooms and parked cars.

The box was filled with plastic bags of marijuana.

Leigh sat back on her heels. She looked around the room. There must have been forty boxes. Her legally trained mind began to function. She remembered gathering information on a nationwide drug sting operation for a case a couple of years before. The operation was known as Delta Nine, and an arm of it had extended to Hawaii, especially the Big Island, where the growing and smuggling of marijuana was widespread. After Delta Nine the state of Hawaii had passed a law making all property on which marijuana was grown subject to confiscation by the government.

Immediately she thought of Malcolm in the helicopter, peering down at her among Simon's sugarcane. Leigh had read that marijuana was often grown amid sugarcane to conceal it. What better way to avoid confiscation of one's own property than to grow it on someone else's? Malcolm had not been spying on her that morning. She had merely been in the wrong place at the wrong time while he was checking on his crop.

A shadow fell across her shoulder. Leigh screamed and spun around.

Kalani stood in the doorway.

She was too shocked to speak. Driven by panic, she pushed her way past him out the door. She cleared the three steps in one leap and stumbled toward the road through the trees. He called after her but she did not stop. She reached the road and ran toward Wailani. She had to reach the bungalow before he caught her.

After a moment she slowed down enough to glance behind her. He was not following her.

She was within sight of the bungalow before she realized she had forgotten the milk and eggs outside the marijuana house.

When she burst into the bungalow, Florence was sitting on the bed in her room, a cup of coffee in one hand, going through a stack of newspapers.

"Look what I found in the closet," she said when she saw Leigh. "Some of these are really old."

Leigh went into the room and sank down on the corner of the bed, one leg tucked under her. Her hair clung to the sides of her face and she suddenly felt tired.

"Aunt Florence, I need to know something. It's very important." She took a deep breath and looked around the room, trying to figure out exactly what it was she wanted to ask. "When was the last time you were in Hawaii?"

Florence lowered the paper and blinked at her niece. "The year after Ross died. Four years ago. I only remember that because I went with the Women's Club tour and roomed with Meg and Harriet. The mosquitoes ate Meg alive on Kauai—"

"Did anything weird happen on that trip?"

"Well, my luggage was sent on to Tokyo by mistake, but I got it back in a few days. Or was that the time before? Yes, it must have been, because I seem to remember Ross being very irate about the whole thing."

"Did you come to the Big Island that time?"

"No, this is the first time I've been to the Big Island.

I had always planned to come before, but every time I came to Hawaii Simon was on the mainland, and I didn't really see the point of coming if he wasn't going to be here.''

"Where did you get that olivine necklace? The one you gave me, remember? Wait a minute, I'll go get it from my room—"

"I know which one you mean." Florence was rather irritated. "You asked me the same thing the day we got here. I told you I didn't remember. I still don't."

"Maybe you got it the last time you were in Hawaii. Four years ago."

"No. It's been lying around in my jewelry box a lot longer than that. I hadn't remembered a thing about it until your mother saw it one day and said I was wearing it when I came home from my first trip to Hawaii, years ago." Florence gave Leigh an exasperated look. "Why is it so important where I got it? Or when?"

"Because the guy who was sitting next to me on the plane acted as if he had seen it before. And he looked like he couldn't have been more than four or five the first time you came to Hawaii, so I wondered if you might have bought it on your last trip."

"No."

There was a silence as they looked at each other. Leigh studied her aunt, wondering how much her vague memory could be trusted. Leigh knew that her aunt was sensitive about the subject of her forgetfulness. It had been a family issue for as long as she could remember, and she was sure Aunt Florence was tired of hearing about it. Leigh would not pursue the subject of the olivine pendant. But there was one more question she had to ask.

"Did Uncle Ross ever have a client from Hawaii? Someone who was, maybe, accused of drug dealing?"

"I don't know. He could have. He didn't discuss his touchier cases with me for legal reasons." Florence got up off the bed with a sigh. "Well. It seems forgetfulness runs in this family. I didn't see you bring in the eggs and milk. Did you forget them? Or did you leave them outside?"

Leigh tried to think of an explanation and could not come up with one. "Sorry. I'll go get them."

She left the bungalow and let the screen door bang shut behind her. For a minute she stood at the top of the stairs in the morning sun. How could she go back to that little house to retrieve her groceries? Kalani might still be there. Whatever reason he had for being there, Leigh was sure her presence would not be welcome.

Was he working with Malcolm? Why else would he have gone to that place? Leigh did not like to entertain that possibility, but she always had been one to face facts. It would explain why he hated Simon so much.

And then she saw it. Down there on the bottom step, leaning carefully against the corner, was her brown grocery bag of eggs and milk.

Leigh headed down to the beach for a swim that afternoon. For some reason she did not go to the nearest stretch of shore. Instead, something compelled her to pass by Coral's house.

If she grimly hoped to catch a glimpse of Malcolm

conferring with Coral, she was disappointed. Coral sat on her veranda, which faced the ocean across a narrow road. On the floor in front of her was a large tray covered with a variety of colorful blossoms. Coral was stringing the flowers one by one onto a strand of heavy cotton thread. The veranda railing was draped with a rainbow of completed leis. Emma sat with her on the veranda in a straight-back wooden chair.

Coral looked up from her work as Leigh mounted the stairs toward them.

"Hi," Coral said, and gave Leigh her quiet, friendly smile.

"Hi. Hello, Emma."

The old woman gave Leigh a stiff nod and a grunt.

"Mr. Trowbridge asked me to make some leis for his dinner guests tomorrow," Coral said. "I guess you and your aunt will be there."

"Most likely. Simon and Aunt Florence spend most of their time together."

Coral rose to her feet, selected a white plumeria lei from the veranda railing, and put it around Leigh's neck. She smiled at Leigh's surprised expression.

"They're best when they're fresh."

Leigh gathered the lei into her hands and breathed in the scent of plumeria. "Thank you. It's beautiful." She glanced off at the ocean. "I was on my way down to the beach for a swim. Would you like to come?"

Coral looked at her grandmother and down at the tray of flowers. "I'd love to," she said suddenly. She picked up the tray and went to the railing, where she gathered up the draped leis. "I'll put these in the re-frigerator. Sit down while I go in and change." She went into the house and the screen door banged shut behind her.

Leigh sat down in the chair Coral had vacated and wondered what to make of the girl. Why had she been with Malcolm last night? Was she in love with him? Leigh could not imagine anyone having tender feelings for Malcolm. Did Coral know about his involvement with marijuana? Probably not. Love had no doubt blinded her to the truth.

Leigh looked up at the sound of scuffling feet. Mrs. Akina was passing by on the road in front of the house. She looked up toward the veranda. Her round face broke into a smile of recognition when she saw Leigh and she nodded hospitably as she continued down the road. Leigh watched the tiny woman walk away.

"You know her?"

Leigh jumped. She had almost forgotten Emma's presence on the other side of the veranda. She looked at the old woman, who fixed her with an imperious stare.

"Not really," Leigh answered. "I've met her son, Kalani."

Emma came up out of her chair and was across the veranda to Leigh in a moment. "You stay away from him! He no good!" the old woman hissed.

A cold dread went through Leigh. She looked up into Emma's face. "Why?"

"They caught him with drugs in his boat! He smuggled stuff down to Hilo! He is dangerous. You better stay away—"

The screen door banged. "Grandma!"

Leigh and Emma looked around. Coral came toward

them, visibly upset. She was dressed in a lime-green bathing suit that set off her dusky skin and her fine figure. "What are you telling Leigh?"

" 'Bout Kalani! 'Bout how they found those drugs on his boat."

"That was never proven, Grandma. They released him, remember?"

"No matter! I know who his friends are." This last statement sounded like a taunt.

"Tutu. Please." Coral's tone was plaintive.

Emma's expression softened as she looked at her granddaughter. She took the girl's black hair into her hands and caressed it. Then she threw Leigh a warning look and went into the house.

Leigh stared after her. Emma had answered one of the questions in her mind: Kalani's appearance at the marijuana house that morning had been no accident.

And Coral had defended him against her grandmother's accusations. *So she does know,* Leigh thought. *She knows about Malcolm and it doesn't matter to her.*

She looked up at Coral, who avoided her eyes. "Shall we go down to the beach?" Coral asked brightly, and led the way down the wooden steps.

Leigh and Coral stayed on the beach until the palms cast long shadows across the sand. Their conversation was light and friendly, and not another word was mentioned about Kalani Akina and the trouble connected with him. But it lay between them like a sleeping dog that would leap up and bite the first person silly enough to disturb it.

Leigh leaned back on her elbows, her legs stretched

out on her towel, and surveyed the aquamarine surf beyond her toes.

"Have you lived here all your life, Coral?" she asked.

"Yes. My tutu—my grandmother—would never live anywhere else. She's one of those old Hawaiians who's a part of the land where she was born. If she moved it would be like pulling up an old tree by the roots."

"And you've always lived with her?"

"Ever since my parents died when I was a baby. She's always been good to me. I owe her a lot."

"And you've never been married?"

"No. I was engaged once, when I was nineteen, to a boy my grandmother really liked. The only problem was, *I* didn't like him. He was sweet, but he let my tutu push him around too much. I think that's why she liked him. It was her way of making sure she would never lose me." A strange expression crossed Coral's face.

"So you broke the engagement?"

"Yes. He got work down in Hilo. He was there for eight years." Coral heaved a careful sigh. "But now he's back."

Leigh recognized the long-suffering look on Coral's face. Suddenly it came to her. "It's Derek," she guessed.

Coral nodded. "He wants to take up where we left off. I haven't found the heart to tell him I'm just not interested. My grandmother is encouraging him, and that's no help. It makes me mad because she knows there's somebody else in my life now. But she likes

Derek better, so she's doing everything she can to—''
Coral stopped short. She threw an apprehensive look
at Leigh and busied herself by sifting black sand
through her fingers.

The sun grew orange as it sank toward the hills in
the west. Leigh and Coral gathered up their things and
went back to Coral's house. Leigh said good-bye and
headed toward the bungalow.

As she walked along in the late afternoon light, the
fragrance of flowers and the ocean breeze caressed her
senses. She passed a plumeria tree, heavy with blossoms. She stopped and picked one and slipped it into
her wet hair over her left ear.

She heard footsteps and looked up. Kalani was coming toward her.

He had not seen her yet. Leigh stepped back against
the trunk of the plumeria tree. Panic prickled in her
throat. She had found out about his drug business. She
didn't want to be alone with him, but there was nothing
to protect her from his sight—just this stand of jungle.

He was coming straight toward her. She must have
made a sound, for he looked up sharply.

She broke away from the tree at a dead run, hoping
to reach Coral's house before he caught up with her.

She heard him crashing through the jungle growth
behind her. She tried to run faster, but her legs felt so
weak she could hardly stay on her feet. She felt his
hand close around her arm. Abruptly she was jerked
backward.

She spun around to face him. His bronze face,
gleaming with sweat, was close to hers.

In an instant her terror became anger. She swung

her free hand around and delivered a resounding slap to his face. "Let go of me!" she demanded through clenched teeth. She struggled to free herself, but his powerful grip only tightened around her arm. She hauled off for another slap. Kalani grabbed her other arm and shook her.

"Stop it! Calm down. I'm not going to hurt you! Do you hear?"

"Then why are you chasing me?"

"I'm not! Why are you running away from me like some scared little animal?" He frowned, then suddenly released her. "Don't be afraid of me," he said.

She stepped back. He reached toward her helplessly.

"Maybe you should be afraid of me," she said. "I'm not an expert, but I recognized what was in those boxes this morning. Aren't you afraid I'm going to tell somebody about it?"

The moment she said it she regretted it. She should have known better than to say something so stupid. Kalani's expression grew menacing. "Don't do that," he said. "It'll ruin everything." He stepped toward her and grabbed her wrist. "Promise me you won't say anything to anyone. Not to Simon or your aunt or anyone. Promise me."

She stared up at him. "Don't you realize what you're doing? I don't know how Malcolm talked you into this, but I'm sure it was his idea—"

He let go of her wrist. "Don't pretend to understand something you don't."

For several moments she rubbed her wrist and glared at him. "What were you doing at that house this morning?"

"I can't tell you that."

"Is all that marijuana yours?"

"No."

"Are you and Malcolm working for someone?"

"Don't ask me any more questions. I can't tell you anything. Don't you understand? The more you know, the more danger you'll be in."

Leigh's heart tightened with fear. "From whom?"

"Just take my word for it. Please. I don't want you to get involved. This is something I have to do. Maybe later you'll understand everything."

*I'll understand, all right,* Leigh thought. But as she calmed down she realized that it would not be wise to aggravate him further. She had to pretend to go along with him no matter what she intended to do.

He must have seen a change in her face, for he seemed to relax. His eyes softened. He was studying her.

He reached toward her and untangled the plumeria blossom from the wet brown hair over her left shoulder. "Are you married?" he asked.

"What?"

He stepped closer. "Are you married? Or engaged? It makes a difference, you know."

"A difference in what?"

"In how you wear the flower." He was now standing over her. He looked down. A soft smile played on his lips.

"No, I'm not married," she almost whispered. "Or engaged."

"Then it belongs on the right side." He tucked the

flower into the damp hair over her right ear. The heel of his hand brushed her cheek. She looked up at him.

"There," he said, and smiled into her eyes. Leigh's breath caught in her throat. Kalani's smile faded. Leigh thought she might drown in the depths of his dark eyes. He gazed at her and then seemed to remember himself. He glanced toward the western sky, where the sun had just set. "You'd better get back to the bungalow. It's getting dark."

She moved away from him. She tried to think of something appropriate to say, but nothing came to her. She turned and walked away.

# Chapter Five

Simon had "other commitments" that evening, so Leigh and Florence had dinner in their bungalow. The freezer was stocked with a variety of meats, and Florence claimed to have a wonderful recipe for chicken, so she shooed Leigh out of the kitchen and said she would call her when dinner was ready.

Leigh wandered out to the veranda. A wash of light still lingered in the sky over the Kohala Mountains. Crickets chirped in the tropical night.

She sat down in one of the chairs and put her feet up on the railing. Now would be the time to write that letter she had promised her mother, she supposed, but it was one of the last things she felt like doing. *Dear Mom,* she would write. *Remember that eminently eligible lawyer I didn't marry because I didn't love him? Remember how worried you were that I'd end up an old maid? Not to worry. I've finally fallen in love. You'll really like him, he's a professional man. He's a drug smuggler. . . .*

A stack of newspapers sat on the other chair. Idly, Leigh picked up the top one, a Hilo newspaper. She perused the front page. Near the bottom was a grainy photograph of a wrecked bus lying on its side on a steep hill. At the top of the slope was a highway and a broken guardrail. The headline of the accompanying article read, BUS ACCIDENT KILLS 12, INJURES 15. She began to read the story.

> *Mud washed onto the highway by seasonal rains was responsible for the crash of a commuter bus on its way from Hilo to Kamuela yesterday. The bus hit a mud slick as it rounded a curve and skidded out of control, crashing through the guardrail and plunging down the side of the hill. Many passengers were thrown free of the bus. One of these was killed. He has been identified as Moekane Akina, proprietor of the former York estate in Hamakua. Eleven people inside the bus were killed. . . .*

Leigh stared at the name. Moekane Akina. She had seen that name before, on a headstone. *He was my uncle,* Kalani had said.

Leigh looked at the date at the top of the page. The newspaper was almost twenty-seven years old. It must have been from the stack of newspapers Aunt Florence had found in the closet that morning. Leigh remembered that George had said this bungalow had been used for storage.

She glanced at the name again. *Moekane Akina, proprietor of the former York estate in Hamakua. . . .* The York estate was Wailani. So Kalani's uncle had owned Wailani. How did Simon get it?

"Dinner's ready!" Florence sang as she pushed open

the screen door with a large tray in her hands. On the tray were two steaming plates, flatware, and napkins. She came across the veranda and set the tray down on the wicker table. "Chicken divan and rice!" she announced proudly. "I had to make a couple of substitutions with the seasonings, but I think it turned out pretty well."

Leigh sniffed appreciatively. "It smells great."

"Thanks. I'll be right back. Would you please move those newspapers off the chair?" Florence went back inside and returned shortly with two glasses of white wine. Leigh scooped the papers on the floor.

"I thought it would be nice to eat out here on the veranda," Florence said. "Such a balmy night. So tell me, Leigh, as long as we have this evening to ourselves, are you ever going to end your mother's torment and get married?"

"Oh, Aunt Florence, not you too."

"Now don't get defensive, dear, it's just a nosy, idle question. Unlike your mother, I don't think there's anything wrong with a woman remaining single, if that's what she wants."

"Well, that's just it. It isn't what I want, not really. I'd like to be married, but it's just so hard to find the right person."

Florence nodded thoughtfully as she stabbed a chunk of chicken. "I can see why. You're intelligent and independent. Pretty as you are, it's a combination that daunts many young men. You're going to have to find someone who isn't afraid of your brains. He's going to be hard to find."

"But that isn't enough. He'd have to take my breath away. Otherwise I just wouldn't be interested."

For a long time Florence said nothing. Leigh supposed her aunt disapproved of setting such a standard for a prospective husband. So her aunt's next words surprised her.

"Then don't settle for less. It's worth waiting for."

Leigh looked at her. Florence gazed out at the night, her wineglass poised in her hand.

"As much as I loved your uncle Ross, I never quite felt that way about him. I always felt there was some grand passion in my life that I had missed."

Leigh studied her aunt with new awareness. She had grown up thinking of her as sweet, proper, sometimes silly Aunt Florence. It had never really occurred to her that Florence had once had the same problems and prospects as she. "It's not too late," Leigh said. Then, slyly, "How do you feel about Simon?"

Florence pressed her lips together. "Finish your dinner."

They finished eating and Florence began gathering the dishes together.

"Oh, don't do that," Leigh said. "I'll do the dishes."

"No, you won't. I've seen the way you clean up." She went inside with her tray of dirty dishes.

Leigh wandered to the veranda railing. The night seemed quiet, but as she listened, the subtle background noises unfolded to her ear—the chirping of the crickets, the distant rumble and hush of the surf. And another sound, faint yet distinct. A rambling tune picked out on the strings of a guitar.

She leaned over the railing, straining to listen. It was coming from the beach. It sounded solitary, as if the player sat on his back porch, head bent over the instrument, his fingers searching for a new melody.

Leigh sat on the railing and listened. She could see him clearly in her mind. *Come to me, enfold me. . . .*

In the middle of the night a crash roused Leigh from a deep sleep. She jumped out of bed and stood swaying in the middle of the room while her brain cleared.

"Leigh!"

Florence's distressed cry propelled her to her aunt's room. Florence sat up in bed. Her lamp was on. Shards of glass glinted on her bedspread. There was a small cut on her cheek. A jagged hole gaped in the glass of the unshuttered window.

"Aunt Florence!" Leigh ran to her aunt. "What happened?"

For a moment Florence sat quite still. Then she began to shake—at first just a tremor, which grew more violent until the bed frame was squeaking. "A rock!" she screamed. "A big sharp rock! Hitting me!"

Leigh threw her arms around her aunt and held her until the shaking subsided. Then Florence sighed deeply and dropped her head against Leigh's shoulder.

Leigh laid her back on the pillow and searched the floor. Near the leg of the bed, half hidden by the spread, was a stone. Leigh picked it up. Written on its flat side was, *Get out,* haole. *Go home.*

"What is it, dear?"

Leigh looked at her aunt. Florence surveyed the glass on her bed with blinking wonder.

Leigh ran out of the room to the front door and outdoors to the drive. The crescent moon overhead shed little light and Leigh strained her eyes in the darkness. Perhaps whoever had thrown the rock was still nearby, hiding. At the moment Leigh was more angry than frightened.

"Where are you?" she shouted. "If you have something to tell me, come here and say it to my face!"

Her words resounded in the darkness. Silence followed them. "Coward!" she cried.

From behind her, down the drive, she heard the faraway drone of an engine coming toward her. She turned. Headlights bounced through the darkness.

A moment later Simon's Land-Rover appeared around the curve. It screeched to a halt beside Leigh.

"Leigh!" Simon exclaimed, leaping out from behind the steering wheel. He wore a business suit and tie. "What are you doing out here in your nightgown? It's almost two in the morning!"

Quickly she explained what had happened.

"Come on. Let's go see if your aunt's all right," Simon said.

Florence, in her robe and slippers, was sweeping the broken glass into a pile on the carpet when Leigh and Simon came in. She looked up. "Why, Simon—"

He went to her and put his arms around her. "Florence, darling, are you all right?"

She seemed a bit flustered by his embrace and gently pushed him away. "Physically, yes. I just don't know if I'll be able to sleep anymore tonight."

"May I see that rock?"

She handed it to him. He read the words with a small frown between his dark brows. He looked up.

"Get dressed, both of you. Pack an overnight bag with whatever you'll need for the next few days. I'll take you up to the house. I'll send a man down here tomorrow to fix the window and clean up. Hurry, now."

Neither Leigh nor Florence raised an objection. As quickly as they could, they dressed and packed and went out to Simon's waiting car, only too glad to get away from the lonely isolation of the bungalow.

## Chapter Six

Leigh did not sleep well for the rest of the night, and the next morning she awoke early. It was raining. The dripping foliage of Wailani was vivid green. Outside the window raindrops rolled off the broad leaves of some exotic tree.

At the breakfast table a short while later, Leigh watched through the windows as the rain swept across the valley. At the head of the table, Simon noisily clinked his spoon in his coffee cup, making no effort to conceal his agitation.

"Who might have done such a thing?" he demanded of them. "You haven't been here long enough to make any enemies. What would possess someone to do something so childish?" He gave Leigh a keen look. "Any ideas, Leigh? Maybe one of the locals doesn't like you. Maybe you've made someone jealous? Taken away somebody's boyfriend?"

His manner irritated her. With great effort she managed to stay calm. "No. I haven't taken away anyone's boyfriend." She thought of Debbie Overgaard. She could picture that girl hurling a rock through somebody's window. But she did not think Debbie was responsible for what had happened last night. Leigh believed it had something to do with what she had discovered in the marijuana house. That meant someone connected with the house had thrown the rock—someone who wanted them gone.

Simon's voice brought her out of her thoughts. "Well, something's got to be done. I will not have my guests harassed with such dangerous pranks. I think the best thing would be for you to stay here for the rest of your visit. I'll drive you down to the bungalow a little later so you can get the rest of your things."

Florence set down her coffee cup. "But I really enjoy staying in the bungalow, Simon. We're close to you and yet we have our privacy too, and we're not in your way. I'd really like to go back once the window's fixed."

Simon and Leigh both stared at her. Leigh was surprised to hear her aunt express such a preference. She had thought Florence would be happy to leave the bungalow, especially if it meant she would be closer to Simon.

"Florence, you can't be serious," Simon said. "What's to prevent the same idiot from doing it again?"

"I left my shutters open last night. I'll keep them closed from now on. Besides, it probably won't happen again. You said it was probably a prank. I don't think we should give whoever it was a sense of power by upsetting our arrangements. Do you?"

"Aunt Florence. . . ."

Florence smiled playfully at her niece. "What's the matter, Leigh, are you going to let one little rock scare you away? Where's that gutsy spirit your mother's always so worried about?''

''But what if this isn't just a prank? Maybe they'll do something more serious next time.'' Leigh looked to Simon for concurrence. His deep-set eyes scrutinized her.

''Oh, come now. There's no reason anyone would want to get rid of us.'' Florence glanced from Simon to Leigh. ''Is there?''

Leigh hesitated. *You have to tell them,* she thought. *Tell them about Kalani and Malcolm and what you found in that little house. If they're growing it on Simon's property, he has a right to know.*

At that moment Coral and Derek came through the swinging door into the dining room, each carrying a tray that they set down on the buffet behind Leigh.

Simon was suddenly gruff. ''You know who threw that rock through your aunt's window last night, don't you?''

From the buffet behind her there was the sharp clatter of silverware. Leigh jumped but did not turn around. ''No, I don't,'' she said angrily. ''Anyway, you're probably right, Aunt Florence. It was just a prank. Let's move back to the bungalow as soon as the window is fixed. Okay?''

Florence regarded her a moment longer and then lifted her coffee cup to her lips. ''All right,'' she said.

Leigh concentrated on rubbing the condensation off her water glass. She would not look at Simon. There was a long silence, broken only by the clinking of dishes as Coral and Derek replaced them in the buffet.

Not until they had finished and left the room did Simon put both hands on the table and push back his chair.

"Well. As soon as you ladies are finished, I think we should go for a ride. The rain seems to be letting up a bit. Would you like to drive down to Honoka'a to see the macadamia nut factory?"

"That would be lovely," Florence said. "Meg and Harriet wanted me to bring them back some chocolate-covered macadamia nuts, and now would be the perfect time to get them. Doesn't that sound like a nice jaunt, Leigh?"

"Sounds thrilling." Leigh caught herself and threw an apologetic glance at Florence. There was no need to take out her irritation with Simon on her aunt. "I'm sorry. I guess I'm a little edgy. I just don't think I'm up to a macadamia nut factory today. You two go ahead. I have some letters to write. Simon, is there anyplace in Honola'i where I can mail them?"

"There's a mail pickup at Akina's General Store once a week. But that's not until Monday. I can mail them for you in Honoka'a if you like."

"I'm afraid they're not written yet."

Simon reached into his pocket and pulled out his keys. He peeled two off the ring and laid them on the table in front of her. "These are to the Land-Rover. You can drive in to Kamuela when you're through with your letters and mail them there. That'll give you a chance to see Parker Ranch. It's the second-largest privately owned ranch in the United States."

"But, Simon, I can't take your Land-Rover—"

"Of course you can. You're my guest here, Leigh, I want you to enjoy yourself. And you're right. Macadamia factories are for old fogies like me''—he shed a charming smile on Florence—''and our long-suffering companions.''

Leigh did not argue further. The truth was, she desperately needed to get away on her own for a while. She picked up the keys. ''Thanks, Simon.''

He gave her a disarming smile and she felt her irritation evaporate. He really was a charming man. She could see why her aunt had fallen for him.

The Land-Rover sped northward along the highway that followed the Hamakua coast. Heavy rolling clouds darkened the sky, but the rain had let up for the moment. The highway twisted and turned through stands of dense jungle and suddenly emerged along a ridge of cliffs that fell away in a rocky tumble to the pounding ocean far below.

Leigh's thoughts were in turmoil as she guided the Land-Rover around the bends in the road. What did a woman do when the man she couldn't get out of her heart had connections with someone who was possibly trying to harm her? Did she go to the police and send them both to jail? Or did she remain silent and wait to be hurt, possibly killed?

Would Kalani protect her from Malcolm?

The highway plunged back into the jungle and came out once more at the top of the ridge. Leigh saw a sign—KAPU LOOKOUT. She pulled off the highway and parked the Land-Rover. She couldn't concentrate on her driving anymore. She had to get out and move around.

Leigh went to stand at the railing that edged the cliff. She looked down and caught her breath.

Jagged green cliffs plunged a thousand feet to the tiny stretch of rocky coastline. Waterfalls cascaded down the faces of the cliffs and were swallowed up in the dense jungle of the gully far below. At the foot of the valley a cove nestled between two arms of black lava rock. A reef extended across the mouth of the cove; beyond it the ocean flung itself against the rocks and burst into vicious white spray. The cloud-laden sky deepened the colors and gave a strange, shrouded aura to the scene.

A movement on the face of the far cliff caught her eye. At first Leigh thought it was another waterfall. But as she watched, incredulous, a piece of the cliff itself slowly slid and then plummeted to the floor of the valley. It left behind a deep red gash on the face of the cliff.

*It's bleeding,* Leigh thought as she stared at the gash. *Even the mightiest cliffs are vulnerable. Why did I think I would be any different?*

Leigh heard a car pull up behind her. She turned. It was Kalani's Bronco. He emerged from it while she stared at him. It was as if she had conjured him up with her thoughts.

He came over to her and glanced around. "Are you alone?"

"Yes."

"I'm just coming back from Kamuela," he said. "I saw you, and I. . . ."

She looked up at him. He looked handsome in a dark-blue knit pullover with the University of Hawaii logo in white on the left side. She looked away, out over the breathtaking valley she had discovered. ''I was on my way to Kamuela and decided to pull over for a look.''

He stood beside her. ''This is Kapu Valley. In ancient times it was taboo, or *kapu,* under Hawaiian holy law. It's inaccessible by land and even by sea on stormy days like today, unless the skipper is familiar with the ins and outs of the reef. Otherwise a boat would break up on those rocks.''

Leigh glanced at him. ''Are you familiar with the reef?''

He nodded. ''I've taken my boat in there a few times. Not many people know about it. The mouth of the cove is so narrow that it's almost invisible from the sea.''

A movement caught Leigh's eye. She pointed. ''Look over there on that far cliff! A little while ago, a big chunk of earth came loose and fell all the way down to the floor of the valley.''

''That happens sometimes if there's been a lot of rain. The soil gets soggy and heavy and finally slides down the hill. On other parts of the islands, houses and people and cars are buried in the mudslides. That never happens in Kapu Valley. No one down there to bury.''

A shudder went through Leigh. Kalani's hand came up to her back in a protective gesture.

''Are you all right?'' he asked.

His large hand spread a pool of warmth across her back. *Be careful,* she warned herself. *Be very careful.*

''Someone threw a rock through my aunt's bedroom

window last night,'' she said. ''Someone doesn't want us here.''

A strange look crossed Kalani's face. ''Does Simon know?''

''Of course. He came and rescued us. We're staying with him now.''

''Is your aunt all right?''

''She's fine. She's almost forgotten it by now. As readily as she forgets most unpleasant things.''

''And how are you?''

''Confused. A little frightened.''

''Confused about what?''

She looked up at him. There was a strange light in his eyes. What was he doing up here, anyway? Why did he have that look on his face?

Instinctively, she took a step back, and hit the railing. She felt herself lose her balance and start to fall backward.

In a moment that lasted a lifetime, Leigh felt herself tumbling over the railing. She saw Kalani's face, saw his hands coming toward her, felt the floor of Kapu Valley a quarter of a mile below her back, coming up to meet her. She screamed.

Kalani lunged for her and pulled her away from the edge, into his arms. Terrified, Leigh clutched him around the waist. She began to shake and could not stop.

Kalani pressed her against his chest, where she could feel his heart beating as furiously as her own. His hand stroked her hair, ''Shh. It's all right. I've got you, Leigh. It's all right.''

She closed her eyes as his hand on her hair soothed

her. Slowly her shaking subsided. She melted into his arms and listened to the comforting beat of his heart. Gradually, she felt his touch change.

She tilted her head back, knowing his lips were just above her head, knowing she was a fool and not caring. He kissed her and she grew dizzy. Leigh knew she was falling, farther and deeper than the Kapu Valley. Yet she was no longer afraid, as long as she was in his arms.

Suddenly Kalani wrenched himself away from her and backed away. Leigh stared at him, surprised and disappointed.

"I'm sorry," he choked. "I can't—I'm sorry." He turned away. Leigh reached out to him.

"Kalani—"

He closed his eyes as if in pain. "I'm sorry. I hope one day soon you'll understand." Blindly he made his way toward the Bronco. He climbed in and started the motor and backed out onto the highway.

Leigh stood with her back to Kapu Valley, alone and desolate, and watched him drive away.

Simon and Florence returned from Honoka'a that evening in time for dinner. Leigh sat at the table with them and smiled and made small talk and found it impossible to think of anything but Kalani. As soon as dinner was over and her aunt and Simon had moved to the living room for coffee, Leigh slipped out the French doors at the end of the dining room.

A flagstone walkway led around the house, lit at regular intervals by foot-high pagoda lights. Leigh followed it, eager to put distance between herself and the occupants of the house and be alone with her thoughts.

The grounds around the house were exquisitely land-scaped and, after dark, artfully lit. Hidden floodlights in green and amber accented a tree here, an outcropping of lava rock there, a bush farther on.

Toward the back corner of the house, however, the landscape lighting disappeared, and Leigh found her-self in near-total darkness. She looked off toward the sea. For a moment she saw nothing but an impenetrable black void.

Then she saw it—the piercing flash of the lighthouse strobe at Point Maka'u. *Maka'u* meant danger, Simon had told them. Or fear. An appropriate name for Leigh's state of mind.

He hoped that one day soon she would understand, Kalani had said. She had no idea what he meant. All she knew was that she ached for her Hawaiian prince, and that frustration was turning to anger inside her.

Out in the black night, the bright flash came again and disappeared. Then, below it, Leigh saw another light—smaller, dimmer, moving erratically. She strained forward and shielded her eyes from the lights behind her.

She could see it clearly now. A tiny pinprick of light—no, two. Three. Several. Bobbing, dancing, dis-appearing, and showing once again. Like the pattern of light that would be made by a small group of people searching for something with flashlights in their hands.

The lighthouse flash swept across Leigh's line of vision and she lost the pinpricks of light. She waited for her eyes to readjust to the darkness. What were they doing out there? There was nothing on that point of land but scruffy grass and an automated lighthouse.

"Leigh?"

She whirled around. Simon drew back at her reaction. She laughed weakly.

"I'm sorry! I wasn't expecting anyone. Simon, is it low tide now?"

He studied her oddly, then glanced out toward the dark ocean. "I believe so, yes. Why do you ask?"

Leigh pointed past him. "Look out there toward the lighthouse. It looks like there are people with flashlights down there."

"Oh, no." His voice was filled with dread. He suddenly looked pale and drawn. "That's it. The pickup. It's happening tonight."

"Pickup? What do you mean?"

"I mean drug smuggling, my dear. Akina's slicker than I thought. I'd better call the authorities right away." He turned toward the house. Leigh grabbed his arm.

"Akina! You mean Kalani?"

Simon stopped and studied her face. "Yes."

"Don't call the authorities—" It was out of her mouth before she had time to think. It was her heart speaking, not her head.

Simon grabbed her shoulders. "What do you know about this? Has he told you anything?"

"No!" Leigh shrugged Simon's hands off her shoulders. "He hasn't told me anything."

He regarded her shrewdly. "Are you in love with him?"

She neatly sidestepped his question. "I've been here only four days. I hardly know him."

"Then you can't know what he's capable of. I'm sorry, Leigh. I have to do this." He turned to go and she clutched his arm again. "If you truly didn't think your Kalani was involved in any of this, you would have no objections to my calling the authorities," he said. "You suspect him too, don't you?"

Leigh stood, silent and still.

"I'm sorry," he said kindly. "But I really have no choice. Though it may be too late now—it looks as if they've already cast off." He turned and hurried toward the house.

After he had left, Leigh looked once again toward the point. The pinpricks of light were gone; out on the water was a tiny red light, as on the starboard prow of a boat.

Leigh knew she should not try to protect Kalani. If he was running drugs then he was hurting people, and she should just let him twist in the wind. But she could not. Somehow, she simply could not.

## Chapter Seven

By the next morning the rain clouds were gone and the day was brilliant. At the breakfast table Simon announced that he was going to take them to Volcanoes National Park.

"You know, the day's perfect for the beach," Leigh said. "I can feel it tugging at me. I hope you don't mind, and I appreciate the invitation, but I think I'll pass up the volcanoes and work on my tan."

Simon and Florence exchanged glances. Leigh saw instantly that they wanted very much to be alone. Leigh was happy that Florence's love life was faring better than her own.

"You're sure?" Florence asked, as if she hoped Leigh were very sure.

"Yes. I want to be brown as a coconut when we go back to Los Angeles."

"Did you pack your swimming things when we left the bungalow the other night?"

"No. I'll go down and change on my way to the beach."

"With any luck the mess will be cleaned up by the time you get there," Simon said. "I sent George into

Kamuela this morning for a pane of glass. He should be down at the bungalow replacing it by now.''

After breakfast Florence went upstairs to get ready for her outing with Simon. Leigh could barely contain her anxiety until her aunt had left the room. She turned to Simon with the question that had kept her awake most of the night.

''What happened after you called the authorities?''

He shook his head. ''It was too late. By the time they got out there everyone was gone. Not a trace left behind. I told you he's slippery. The trick is to catch him with his hands on the stuff.'' His voice grew confidential. ''Please take the advice of an old man who's been around the block a few times. Stay away from Kalani Akina. I realize he's an astonishing specimen of young manhood, but he's been bad news as far back as I can remember. Believe me, Leigh. He just isn't worth it.''

*All very easy for you to say,* Leigh thought. *He's never taken you in his arms at the edge of a precipice.*

After Simon and Florence had left for the park, Leigh walked down to the bungalow to get her swimming things. Apparently George had already been there. Florence's window was repaired and the shards of glass had been swept off the veranda. When Leigh went inside she found a note on the bed of Florence's bare room: *Clothes and things are in small room. Made it easier to clean up glass in here. George.*

Leigh went back to her tiny room. It was even more of a mess than usual. Florence's suitcases lay about on the floor, her toilet articles crowded the top of the chest of drawers, and her old stack of newspapers sat on the unmade bed. As Leigh's eyes adjusted to the gloom she found her blue-and-green bathing suit in the chest of drawers. She changed into it and found her terry-cloth cover-up in a small white heap on the floor.

As she pulled the cover-up over her head she heard a noise. She stopped. For a moment she could hear nothing but her own breath through the terry-cloth.

Then she heard it again. The creak of a floorboard. She stood still, listening. There it was again. It came from the veranda. Someone was out there.

Leigh's heart pounded in her ears. *He's here,* she thought. *Whoever threw that rock is back to make sure we're gone.*

Suddenly her fear gave way to anger. *I'll show him we're not gone,* she thought. She ran out of the room to the front door and burst out onto the veranda.

"What do you think you're doing here?" she shouted.

And ran straight into Kalani.

She stumbled backward and stared at him. He was clearly as startled as she was.

"You!" she gasped. "What are you doing here?"

He glanced at the new pane of glass in Florence's window. "I came by to see how things were going," he said. "I didn't expect you to be here."

"That was obvious." She stared up at him. His expression grew cold.

"What are you thinking?"

"What am I supposed to think?" she cried. "I don't know what you want from me. Yesterday you made me feel things I've never felt. But every time I open myself up, you walk away. You're not going to do that to me again. It's about time I got my head clear about you. You expect me to keep my mouth shut about your little marijuana house and your dealings with that creep Malcolm. And to make sure I do, you go so far as to kiss me and turn me to butter, and I can't say anything, not even last night when—''

He took two long strides toward her. "Is that what you think? That I kissed you to keep your mouth shut?''

"What am I supposed to think? I should have gone to the police about that marijuana house days ago.''

"No—''

She turned on him. "Maybe if I had, there wouldn't have been all that activity at Point Maka'u last night.''

Kalani blinked. "What activity?'' He grabbed her wrist.

"I saw it from Simon's house last night. Some lights and a boat down at the point. Simon said you were out there making a pickup. He called the authorities but they were too late.'' She looked up into his face. "Simon says he's been trying to catch you for a long time. But you're slicker than he thought. Those were his words.''

Kalani released her wrist and began to laugh. He turned away and walked across the veranda. His laughter was mirthless and bitter. "Of course he would say that! So he called the authorities, huh? What authorities?''

"I don't know.''

"Did you see them?''

"No. Simon left the house to take care of it. I didn't see him again until this morning.'' Leigh regarded the tall, broad-shouldered man across the sunlit veranda. "You hate him, don't you?"

Kalani looked away.

"In your place I would feel the same way," she said.

He gave her a strange look. "What do you mean?"

"I know your uncle owned Wailani before Simon did. My aunt found an old newspaper in the closet with an article about the bus crash that killed your uncle. They called him 'the proprietor of the former York estate.' Was that true?"

"Yes."

"How did Simon get it? Why didn't it go to your father when your uncle died?"

Kalani turned to face her. The white T-shirt he wore stretched across his chest. His large brown hands gripped the railing behind him.

"All right, I'll tell you," he said. "There are too many things I can't say. But at least I can tell you this.

"Uncle Moekane and Simon met in the Navy. They were both eighteen and they became best friends, closer than brothers. At the time my father wasn't even born yet. He and Uncle Moekane were over twenty years apart.

"When Simon and Uncle Moekane got out of the Navy they both enrolled at the University of Hawaii on the GI Bill. My uncle majored in geology and Simon went into pre-law. I guess his law studies gave him the idea to make out wills together. Most sailor buddies just get tattooed together, but not them. They went to a lawyer and had wills drawn up, legal and binding, and they left all their worldly possessions to each other.

They added a clause invalidating the will if either of them had children, but at the time neither of them was planning on that at all. Anyway, the wills didn't mean much at the time because neither of them had anything of value. To them those wills were a pact of friendship.

"Simon got married right after he graduated from the university, but it didn't last very long. My uncle Moekane never got married, so their friendship stayed close for years. Uncle Moe became a professor of geology at the University of Hawaii and Simon became a successful lawyer. Then a woman named Phoebe York Hampton died. Do you know who she was?"

"The last of the York family. She's buried at Wailani."

"Yes. She was an only child and she and her husband never had children. She outlived her husband, and at the end of her life, she found herself with no one to leave her estate to. So she left it to the eldest son of the only man she had ever really loved."

It took Leigh a moment to put this together. "Your grandfather?"

Kalani nodded. "His name was David Akina. He and Phoebe were in love when they were young, but her father wasn't about to let his daughter marry a Hawaiian. So she married Seth Hampton and my grandfather married my grandmother, a Chinese girl.

"I guess Phoebe came to think of my uncle as the child she wished she'd had. So when she died she left everything to Uncle Moe."

"And because of the will he'd made, it all went to Simon when he was killed in the bus crash."

"That's right. My uncle had forgotten about that

will. It had never been very important, until he inherited the York estate. My uncle and Simon were still pretty close then. It wasn't until a few years later that their friendship ended.''

"Ended? Just like that? What happened?''

Kalani shook his head. He looked troubled. ''It's too complicated to go into. Anyway, when Uncle Moe first inherited the York estate he used to come back to the Big Island all the time, whenever he had time off from the university. But he had to live on Oahu because of his work, and as my father got older he started looking after Wailani more and more in my uncle's absence. By the time he was nineteen he felt like he owned the place. Uncle Moe told my father he was going to make a will and leave everything to him. But after he died no one could find the new will. So the old will stood.''

Leigh turned things over in her mind. ''So you and your family should be living in that house. Not Simon. No wonder you feel the way you do.''

"I don't resent him over that house, only about the way he treated my uncle. He turned on him, and then accepted his property anyway. I resent what he did, not what he has.'' He looked away.

Leigh watched him. His strong profile was bronze against the blue sky. ''Does your father feel the same way you do?''

"My father carries around more anger than I do. He has more reason.''

"And your mother?''

His head snapped toward her. There was no denying the anger in his eyes. ''My mother died when I was born. The woman you saw at the store is my step-mother. She came to Hawaii from the Philippines and met my father when I was five.''

''Was your mother Hawaiian?''

There was a long silence. ''My mother was a *haole* girl.''

The whisper of the ocean came to them on a soft breeze. Leigh stared at Kalani. Finally he smiled.

''I look just like a *haole,* don't I?''

''Well, I never would have guessed, but now that you mention it. . . .''

Kalani started to laugh. He was really quite attractive when he did so. Leigh could not help but laugh with him.

He pushed away from the railing. ''I'd better go. I'm supposed to be helping my father at the store.'' He headed for the steps.

''Did you really come here just to see if everything was all right?''

He paused and turned to her. ''Yes. But as long as you're here, I have a confession to make. You were right. I should never have kissed you. That was a mistake.''

He turned once again for the stairs. Halfway down he looked back. ''But not for the reason you think.''

He left, and again Leigh stood alone and watched him go. That was one confession she could have done without.

Leigh went down to the beach for a swim, but she didn't go far out into the water since the surf was still rough after yesterday's storm. She spent most of her time stretched out on her towel on the black sand, thinking about what Kalani had told her.

His uncle and Simon had been the best of friends. Simon had inherited Wailani from Moekane. What had happened to end their friendship? Kalani had not told her everything, and Leigh was crazy with curiosity.

After a couple of hours she picked up her towel and went back to the bungalow to change. Then she moved Florence's things back to her room and put them in order. Neatness was so important to her aunt. Her own room she left exactly as it was.

Simon had told her she could go horseback riding whenever she liked. It seemed a great way to spend the afternoon, so she headed back through the trees toward the verdant valley below Simon's house.

The valley came into view, a spot of green serenity crowned by the giant banyan at its center. Leigh strolled across the meadow toward the stables on the far side.

As she passed into the shade of the banyan tree, Leigh glanced off to her right. A movement caught her eye. Someone was in the York family burial plot.

The person was kneeling, partially obscured by the headstones. Leigh stopped. A moment later a woman rose. She was in her early sixties, chic and well-groomed, wearing a dark-blue suit and heels.

She had not seen Leigh. She backed away and looked down at one of the graves with a misty smile on her face. Then she turned and headed away across the valley toward the road.

Leigh watched her until she disappeared through the dense foliage that separated Wailani from the main road. Her visit to the gravesite had obviously been clandestine.

Overcome with curiosity, Leigh headed for the burial plot. She passed the headstones of Phoebe York, her husband, and her father, and came to a stop at a grave on which a bouquet of fresh anthurium rested.

The inscription on the stone was brief. It simply read, S. TROWBRIDGE.

## Chapter Eight

Leigh and Florence moved back into the bungalow the next day. That evening at seven o'clock, Simon pulled up in his Mercedes to take Florence to a formal fund-raiser dinner in Hilo. Simon cut a cool, elegant figure in his tuxedo. He handed Florence a square box containing a white orchid corsage, which he pinned to her lavender silk gown. Leigh had not seen her aunt so lovely—or happy—in a long time.

Leigh watched Simon quietly. Why had he never mentioned the grave with his name on it? Who was buried under that headstone?

After she watched them drive off, Leigh hurried to get ready for the party at the Akina house. George would be there in half an hour to pick her up.

She stood before the mirror and brushed her hair to a sheen with long, slow strokes. She had put on a white muslin dress with an off-the-shoulder neckline and a beaded belt of aquamarine blue. The white of the dress looked good against her new tan. When she had finished brushing her hair, she picked a white plumeria blossom to put over her right ear.

When she heard the roar of George's Jeep coming

up the drive, she grabbed her purse, took a last look in the mirror, and hurried out the front door, slamming it behind her.

George jumped out of the Jeep and started toward the bungalow. He wore yellow slacks and a short-sleeved white dress shirt that was clearly visible in the deepening dusk. So was the flash of his smile when he saw Leigh come down the stairs.

"Hi," he said, and opened the Jeep door for her. "You look great."

"Thanks. You're not so bad yourself." She climbed into the passenger seat. "George, can I ask a big favor of you?"

"Sure."

"Can we go pick up Coral? I don't think she wants to show up at the party by herself."

George started up the Jeep. "No problem. You mean she's not going with her boyfriend?" Sarcasm dripped from his voice.

"You mean Derek? She wouldn't go with him if—"

"No. I mean that other jerk. Malcolm."

"So you know about Malcolm."

"Yeah. Everybody knows about them, even though it's supposed to be some dark secret. Her grandmother hates him. I can't blame the old lady."

"She wants Coral to renew her engagement to Derek."

"Yeah. Lucky for Coral she got out of that one. Derek's a nice enough guy, but he's not real smart, you know? He can't make any decisions on his own.

Just does what everybody tells him to. He wants Coral, though. Wants her bad.''

"I take it you don't think too highly of Malcolm, either.''

"He's weird. He's always coming and going, sneaking in and out of the shadows. Gives me the creeps. His father's some rich dude in Honolulu. Malcolm's got bucks.'' George put the Jeep in gear and they bounced off down the drive.

As they pulled up in front of Coral's house, she came out to the veranda and waved to them.

"I'll be a couple of minutes,'' she called. "Come on up.''

They parked and went up the steps to the veranda. Emma sat in her straight-back chair on the porch. She gave the two young people a shrewd stare with her glittering old eyes.

"You take my Ko'a to the Akina house? For a party? You make sure she stays wit' you, George, or wit' Derek. Derek's a nice boy. Don' let her go off wit' that friend of Kalani's. He's no good. Kalani's no good either. They're in a bad business together. Right, George?''

George shrugged. Emma gave him a sly smile.

"Everybody thinks the old woman don' know nothing, but I know plenty. I see plenty.'' She sat forward in her chair. "So how come you take Ko'a to a party? How come she's not goin' wit' Derek?''

"I don't know—'' George began.

"I invited her to go with us,'' Leigh explained.

"Oh? You invite? Who are you? Is this yo' party? Is that yo' Jeep? Is this yo' island?''

Until this moment Leigh had not thought of it in those terms. Emma's hostility embarrassed her. "No—" she began.

"Next thing you'll be trying to take Ko'a back to the mainland wit' you. Trying to take her away from me."

"No! Really. I'm sorry if I've made you feel that way. Coral and I are friends and I—I—" She felt a hand on her arm and looked at George. He frowned and shook his head and made a subtle circular motion around his ear with his forefinger. Then he gave her one of his reassuring smiles.

Coral came out of the house. "Hi," she said. "I'm ready. Thanks for waiting." She wore a sleeveless pale-green dress with a close-fitting bodice and full skirt. Small white pikake blossoms nestled in her cloud of black curls. Her demeanor was as self-contained as ever, but her dark eyes danced with excitement. She bent over and kissed Emma's cheek. " 'Bye, Grandma. See you after the party."

The three friends went down the steps to the Jeep. Emma rose out of her chair and came to the veranda railing.

"Stay away from that Malcolm!" she warned.

Coral bowed her head and climbed into the back of the Jeep. Leigh got into the front beside George.

As they headed down the road and George commenced his friendly small talk over the roar of the engine, the uneasiness Emma had created among them began to dissipate. All the way to the party George shouted amiably at the two women about his father's new Cadillac and his own plans for a new car. Neither

Leigh nor Coral attempted a reply. Leigh was content to sit and listen to him with the warm breeze in her hair. She knew Coral had her mind on Malcolm, and though she disagreed with Emma's methods, Leigh shared her concern about Coral's attachment to him.

The party was being held on the beach in front of Kalani's house. Tall torches had been thrust into the sand at regular intervals around the perimeter of the site, and their flickering light cast undulating shadows across the sand. Strings of colored paper lanterns criss-crossed overhead among the trees, and closer to the house, band instruments were set up.

George, Leigh, and Coral found some vacant folding chairs under the web of paper lanterns and sat down. Debbie Overgaard came toward them, looking prettier than usual. She flicked a glance across the top of Leigh's head and sat down in an empty chair on George's other side. "There's tons of people here, aren't there? This is gonna be some party. It'll be better when the music starts, then we can dance. You got seats close to the band, right?" she said.

"Yeah. Hey, look, there's your brother and his girl-friend."

"I can't stand dat girl!" Debbie said. "Whenever she's around me, she acts like she smell something *hauna pilau.*"

"Maybe she does," George said with a grin.

Debbie gave him a shove that almost toppled him off the chair. "Hey, you jerk!" she shouted. Several people looked around. George was embarrassed.

"Debbie, not so loud!"

"Bother you?"

George stood up. "I'll be back in a minute," he said to Leigh, and left.

Debbie watched him go toward the house, her arms crossed, a disgruntled frown on her face. Suddenly she looked at Leigh. "I owe you money or something?"

"Calm down, Debbie. George is a nice guy. You should try being a little nicer to him."

"Mind yo' own business! If you don't be careful, somebody's going to throw another rock through yo' window!" Debbie jumped up and flounced off through the crowd toward the house. Leigh stared after her. She and Coral exchanged glances.

"Hi, Coral."

They both looked up. There stood Derek, smiling eagerly. He had exchanged his houseboy's clothes for an exquisitely embroidered blue shirt. He looked scrubbed and combed and very much in love. Leigh felt Coral's quiet exasperation, which did not show at all in her bright greeting.

"Hi, Derek. How long have you been here?"

"About half an hour. I been looking fo' you." He sat down beside her. Leigh, watching him, felt sorry for him. He seemed unaware that he did not have a chance in the world with this girl.

Leigh sat back and looked around. She saw Kalani making his way through the crowd toward the band instruments. He was taller than most of his guests and easy to spot. Red and blue lantern light gleamed off his black hair. He wore black pants and a white dress shirt that was open at the throat; Leigh caught the gleam of a gold chain around his neck. Her pulse quickened.

*He's all wrong for you,* her head told her. But her heart did not believe it.

The last member of the band arrived and the four of them tuned up. Kalani stood behind the double-decker keyboards. Raymond tapped eight counts on the rim of his snare drum and the band came in loud and strong on "Volcano." A rush of energy surged through the party guests and they made their way to the torchlit sand in front of the band to dance.

Derek turned to Coral. "Wanna dance?"

"All right." Only Leigh saw Coral's reluctance as she and Derek joined the other dancers.

Around the perimeter of the party, beyond the light of the lanterns and torches, people loitered in the shadows. One of them was Malcolm. Half obscured by the trunk of a palm, he watched the dancers. He was unaware of Leigh's surveillance. The sardonic expression he had worn on the plane was gone. All defenses were down, and he looked vulnerable.

She followed his gaze. He was watching Coral as she danced with Derek. Leigh turned away. Malcolm's presence at this party disturbed her. Had Kalani invited him? Did Coral know Malcolm was here? How much did Coral really know?

The band played for nearly an hour before they took a break. During that time Leigh watched Kalani from time to time. He was a different person when he played his music—outgoing, playful, even mischievous. There was much that she did not yet know about Kalani Akina.

The guitar player spoke into the microphone. "Thank you very much. We'll take a pause and be back in a few minutes. Meanwhile there will be some recorded music, so keep dancing.''

The members of the band dispersed into the crowd. Leigh watched Kalani. He lingered at the keyboards, greeting a few people as they went by.

The recorded music picked up where the band had left off. A slow, heart-rending song that begged to be danced to came through the speakers. People were immediately up and dancing again, swaying to the music as they held each other close.

''Would you like to dance?''

Leigh looked up. Kalani stood beside her chair. She suddenly knew what the poets meant when they wrote of hearts leaping into throats. She swallowed hers back down to where it belonged and rose out of her chair.

He took her hand and led her to the other dancers. When he turned to slip his arm around her waist, Leigh dropped her eyes. It was one of the few times in her life she had ever felt shy. She placed her hand almost gingerly on his shoulder. Highly tuned to his touch, she followed his lead as they began to move to the music, swaying in a small circle in the sand.

''Thank you for coming,'' he said close to her ear. ''I wondered if you would.''

She looked up into his eyes. He smiled, and Leigh thought it was the kindest, gentlest smile she had ever received. *I could love this man,* she thought, and found herself wishing that he would kiss her again. *He can't be a criminal,* she thought. *There must be some other explanation.*

Her eyes drifted down to his full mouth, and she

grew weak with the memory of his kiss. His lips curved into a different kind of smile.

"So I turned you to butter?" he asked quietly.

She glanced up at his amused eyes. "What?"

"That's what you told me at the bungalow. You said I kissed you and turned you to butter. I've hardly been able to think of anything else since. Nobody's ever described my kisses like that before. I like it."

Leigh felt her face grow hot. She looked away from his laughing eyes. In spite of herself Leigh felt her heart opening wide to admit this man. She felt his breath in her hair and the beating of his heart.

*Be careful, Leigh,* she told herself. *Remember what he said.* The kiss was a mistake. So why was he so warm and gentle? Why did she want to laugh and cry at the same time? Why was she allowing herself to fall in love with him when she knew he would only withdraw?

Because she couldn't help it. No matter what happened tomorrow, she was with him now, and she would savor the moment. A short time to love was better than no time at all.

And so they danced, bodies and souls entwined, until the recordings stopped and it was time for the band to play again.

George was solicitous to Leigh all evening while the band played, as Debbie seethed semisilently on the other side of him. A few times she flounced away and danced with someone else, as if to show George she didn't need him. Leigh wondered if he was playing some cruel little game with Debbie.

Derek stayed close to Coral all evening, and her resigned sweetness grew steadily more desperate. During the third hour of the party she managed to slip away, and Leigh did not see her again for about forty-five minutes. When Coral returned to her seat, she looked calm, smug, secretive. There was a gleam in her eyes and her face was flushed. Leigh glanced back in the direction Coral had come from, from the shadows behind the house. Malcolm. There could be no other explanation.

The band announced its last break. Leigh picked up her purse and hurried toward the house. She was beginning to feel a little wilted and wanted to repair her appearance.

Around the side of the house, behind a tall hedge of shrubbery, a door opened into a small bathroom. Leigh went in and brushed her hair until it hung smooth and shiny down her back. The makeup would take a little longer, but she wasn't going to rush it. She wanted to look her best if Kalani asked her to dance again. Then she heard talking just beyond the shrubbery.

"What's up?" a voice asked quietly.

"We blew it the other night!" another voice hissed. "The shipment left without us!"

"Yeah. When's the next pickup?" the first voice asked.

"Next Saturday."

"Saturday? You know he's having a party Wednesday? Why not then? Good cover-up."

"No, it's Saturday," the second voice said.

"All right, if you're sure. But get there on time next

time! You have to cover my back door or he'll have
both of us!''

"I will, I will. Are any of his scouts here tonight?''
"Yeah, the hotheaded one. Watch out for him.''
"You got it.''
"I'd better get back out there. The guys'll be looking
for me pretty soon. See ya, man.''

Leigh stood frozen behind the wall of shrubbery.
She had heard the whole whispered conversation. One
voice she couldn't be sure of. But there was no mis-
taking Kalani's voice.

She saw him emerge from behind the screen of
bushes and walk off toward the party. He had not seen
her. Her heart felt like lead. All the excuses she had
tried to make for his association with Malcolm turned
to ashes.

Devastated, Leigh started slowly back toward the
party. Then a hand grabbed her arm and whirled her
around. Leigh screamed. Malcolm held her wrist and
his face, close to hers, was a stony mask.

"What did you hear?'' he demanded. "I've been
too careful to blow it like this. You know too much.
What did you hear?''

Terror gripped Leigh. She struggled against him with
more strength than she knew she had, but his grip held
fast. A ragged scream ripped free of her throat.

She heard a yell, felt a jerk, and abruptly Malcolm
released her. She stumbled backward. Malcolm was
on the ground and George straddled him, hitting his
face.

Things began to happen fast. People rushed over.
Coral burst through the crowd and threw herself at

George. She grabbed his hair and pulled him back, crying Malcolm's name. Debbie came at a dead run and jumped Coral, screaming pidgin obscenities.

Leigh was dizzy. Everyone shouted at once. She ran toward Debbie and shoved her away from Coral. Then Derek was there and dragged Coral off George, away from the melee.

Leigh felt two large hands on her shoulders. She looked up. Kalani held her and the look on his face was alarmed, concerned.

"Are you all right?" he asked urgently.

"I—I don't know. . . . Malcolm grabbed me and then George—"

Kalani strode past her to the two men on the ground and pulled George off Malcolm.

George whirled and swiped a blow at Kalani. Kalani's fist split the skin over George's brow. He reeled backward and fell to the ground. Debbie rushed to him.

Kalani went to Malcolm. He leaned over and offered his hand to help him up. As he did so a medallion, suspended from the gold chain around his neck, fell dangling out of his shirt.

It was Florence's olivine pendant.

Leigh's hand went abruptly to her neck, as if to catch something before it was snatched away. She stared at Kalani.

He helped Malcolm up. Malcolm's face was bloody. Kalani moved toward the house, his arm around Malcolm's shoulders. Coral rushed toward them. She put her arm around Malcolm's waist and supported him on the other side. Slowly, the three moved toward the house. As they passed Leigh, Kalani looked at her. His voice was low, remorseful.

"I'm sorry," he said.

Leigh stared after him. Sorry for what? Sorry that Malcolm had frightened her? Or sorry that he, Kalani, had stolen Florence's pendant?

George sat up on the ground. Debbie was at his side. When she saw Leigh, she turned on her.

"This is all yo' fault!" she cried. "You come and start trouble. Everyplace you go bad things happen! Why don' you go home? We don' need you!"

"Shut up, Debbie," George muttered as he clambered to his feet. He pressed the heel of his hand over the bloody gash in his forehead. Debbie clutched his shoulder.

"George, are you okay? Yo' eyebrow is bleeding—" She reached up to touch it. He shook her away.

"Come on," he said gruffly to Leigh. "I'll take you home now. Where's Coral?"

"With them," Leigh said, and nodded toward the three receding figures.

"Oh, no." George stumbled toward them. He caught up to Coral and touched her arm. "We're leaving now—"

Angrily she shook him off. "Get away from me!" she cried. "I don't want a ride from you! I'll find my own way home." She glared at him and then turned back to Malcolm.

George and Leigh rode home in silence. Her mind whirled with everything that had happened this evening and the possible implications.

The pendant. Why did Kalani have it? Was that the

reason he had come to the bungalow yesterday, when he thought no one was there? Had he returned after she'd left and taken it?

Why was it so important?

She looked at George. His face as he drove was set in anger. The bleeding over his eye had stopped, but the cut still showed darkly.

"Thank you," she said.

"For what?"

"For coming to my rescue. For a minute I thought Malcolm was really going to hurt me."

"Somebody should lock that guy up." George glanced at her. "Why did he attack you, anyway?"

Leigh took a breath. "Because I overheard something and he was afraid I was going to tell what I heard."

"What did you hear?"

"I heard him talking to someone about missing the pickup. They said there would be another one on Saturday and to get there on time—"

"Who was he talking to?"

Leigh suddenly realized she had said too much. The hard truth was that if she exposed Malcolm she would expose Kalani as well, and despite the betrayal she felt, she was not yet ready to do that.

"I don't know," she lied. "I couldn't see them, I only heard them."

"Do you have any idea what they were talking about?"

"No."

There was a long silence. Then George chuckled. "Then I guess Malcolm overreacted, didn't he?"

They pulled up in front of the bungalow. Leigh thanked him and started to climb out of the Jeep. Then she turned to him. "Thanks for everything. I'm sorry about your eye."

George touched his eyebrow and winced. "Akina's got a brutal punch." He shrugged. "Are you going to be all right? I don't mind staying with you until your aunt gets back."

"I'll be fine. Good night, George."

He grinned in the darkness. "Lock the door. And close all the shutters!"

Leigh went up the steps and opened the front door as George drove off. She went in and locked it behind her.

His words came back to her. *Akina's got a brutal punch. He also has my aunt's pendant,* Leigh thought as she hurried back to her room. Or a very close copy.

Her room was still the shambles she had left it. Where had she put the pendant? She went to the dresser and began to rummage through drawers. She searched the floor, the closet, her suitcase.

The pendant was gone.

## Chapter Nine

The next day Leigh and Florence boarded the noon flight to Honolulu. Leigh sat in the window seat on the plane and watched the Big Island drop away below them until it was just a green-and-brown smudge in the glassy blue Pacific. She wished her problems could drop away as easily.

Honolulu, she soon discovered, was basically like any other city. As she and Florence followed the Nimitz Highway from the airport toward Waikiki in their rented Lincoln, they passed through Honolulu's industrial section and its low-rent district. But overhead was a clear blue sky; to the north, green-clad mountains lifted their jagged faces; and to the south was the Pacific.

They reached the resort area of Waikiki about half an hour later, driving past shops and restaurants and at least two dozen hotels before they arrived at their own.

The desk clerk in the lobby was gracious and accommodating, and registered them efficiently. Before they left the desk, he handed Leigh a letter.

As the elevator carried them up to the nineteenth

floor, Leigh looked at the envelope the man had given her. Florence looked over her shoulder.

"Somebody found you in a hurry. Who's it from?"

"Dad."

"Grant? Oh, how nice. You will share it with me when we get to the room, won't you?"

"Of course."

Their "room" took Leigh's breath away. The suite consisted of two bedrooms, a bathroom, a kitchenette, and a sitting room. Two sliding glass doors opened onto a balcony that wrapped around the corner of the building. Off to their right was a view of the wrinkled, jewel-green hills above Honolulu; to their left was Waikiki Beach and Diamond Head.

"Aunt Florence, this is incredible!" Leigh exclaimed, with her hands on the balcony railing. A sudden gust of wind came off the water and lifted her long hair off her shoulders. She thought she felt the building sway a bit.

Leigh turned and went back into the sitting room. She settled down on the couch and opened her father's letter. Florence crossed the room to the kitchenette and opened the refrigerator.

"Would you like a Pepsi?" she asked.

"Yes, please. Guess what? Dad says he's flying to Tokyo for a convention and he wants to stop over in Honolulu for lunch on his way. He says he'll be here Wednesday. He wants us to pick him up at the airport and he'll take us to lunch at the Ala Moana Center. Won't that be fun? What's the matter?"

"Don't you remember? We've shortened our stay here so we can get back to the Big Island in time for Simon's party. We're leaving Wednesday morning.''

Leigh studied her aunt's face as Florence brought her a glass of Pepsi. This party of Simon's was so important to her that she was willing to forgo a visit from her brother, of whom she was quite fond. Leigh took a sip of Pepsi as a plan formed in her mind.

"Well, I'm sure it's too late for Dad to change his plans, and I'd love to see him here in Honolulu. I'll tell you what. Why don't I drive you to the airport Wednesday morning? You can catch your flight back to Hilo. Then I can meet Dad for lunch, do a little sight-seeing, and fly to Hilo the next morning. How's that?''

Florence thought about it. Leigh could see she was relieved not to cancel her party plans. "You'll miss the party,'' she said.

"That's all right. I went to a party last night. This one is more yours than mine anyway.''

Florence mulled it over a moment longer, but the decision had already been made. "All right. Thank you, Leigh.'' She gave her a grateful smile. "Now, what do you say we do a little shopping? I noticed a lovely jewelry shop across the street. I really do want to find a coral necklace.''

"Let's go,'' Leigh said.

They left the hotel and crossed Kalakaua Avenue with a crowd of tourists and, once on the other side, headed toward Yamashiro Ltd Honolulu.

The jewelry store was modern, carpeted, and air-conditioned. A glass display case, immaculately clean, ran around three sides of the store, filled with well-

appointed displays of jewelry—everything from dia-
monds to coral. A well-dressed Japanese man of about
thirty-five stood behind the counter, showing a gold
bracelet on a black velvet tray to a customer.

When the woman was through examining the bracelet, he returned it to the display case and locked the
back panel. Then he turned to Florence with a gracious
smile.

"May I help you?"

Florence told him what she was looking for and he
said he believed he had just the thing. He went off and
came back with a white velvet box, which he opened
for Florence.

She gasped. "Oh, Leigh—look." She smiled and
lifted the exquisite necklace out of the box—dozens of
bean-size orange corals in an intricate gold setting.
Florence spread the necklace over her chest and turned
to Leigh. "Isn't it divine?"

She had to admit that it was. "I think they saw you
coming, Aunt Florence."

"They certainly did. Yes, I'll take this. If you'll
wrap it up for me—I'm sorry, what's your name?"

"Kevin."

"If you'll wrap it up for me, Kevin, I'll just browse
over here for a minute. You have a lovely store."

"Thank you." He smiled and turned to Leigh as
soon as Florence was out of earshot. "What a charming
woman."

"Yes, she is. I've seen her charm the quills off
several human porcupines—"

The rest of the words choked off in her throat. She
went numb as she stared at a photograph on the wall

behind Kevin. Three people were in the picture, standing around a cake with the number ten on it, smiling at the camera. One was Kevin; the second was a gray-haired Japanese man. The third was Malcolm.

Leigh blinked. She glanced at Kevin and back at the picture. "Who's that?" she whispered.

"That was the store's tenth anniversary a few months ago. That's me with my father and brother."

"Your brother? Does he work here too?"

"Malcolm? No. He works for one of the airlines. He's gone most of the time. Just comes for visits once in a while. You know him? Hey, are you okay?"

Leigh shook her head. "I—I think I'll just go out for some air. Aunt Florence, I'll meet you outside. In fact, I'll meet you back at the hotel, all right?"

"Are you not feeling well? Oh dear, I should have given you a chance to rest before I dragged you shopping," Florence said.

"No, it's all right, really. I'll see you later." Leigh turned and hurried out of the store.

It had begun to rain. Leigh crossed the glistening street and hurried along the crowded, wet sidewalk. All the way back to the hotel, she glanced over her shoulder to see if she was being followed. She saw no one. Yet she felt as she had that day in the sugarcane field, when Malcolm had flown over in a helicopter. Even here in carefree Waikiki she could not escape his presence.

Leigh returned to the penthouse suite to find that the luggage had been brought up. She took her suitcase into her room and opened it on the bed. As she flipped the lid up, she heard a metallic clink. Curious, she lifted up her clothes from one side of the lid. There, peeking out of a small rip in the lining, was Florence's olivine pendant.

Carefully, Leigh extracted the necklace from its hiding place. She sank down onto the bed, staring at the gray-green rock in her hand.

Now she remembered. She had slipped the pendant into the lid of her suitcase. Somehow, it must have slid into the rip in the lining.

Kalani hadn't taken it after all. It had been in her suitcase all the time. For a moment she was overcome with relief. Kalani wasn't a thief.

Which did not explain why he had been wearing it.

Leigh turned the pendant over. *Souza—Oahu* was imprinted on its smooth gold back. It had been bought in an Oahu shop over a quarter-century ago. No doubt the shop had sold more than one. Kalani's was simply an exact duplicate of Florence's.

Why would two such different people have the same pendant? Why would Kalani have a pendant that was so old? It was as old as he was. . . .

Leigh looked up at the sound of a key in the lock. A moment later the door banged shut, and Florence appeared in the hallway just outside her room, flushed and loaded down with packages.

"I had a marvelous time shopping!" she exclaimed. "Waikiki does have the most charming shops, though you could spend a fortune in them without half trying." Florence continued down the hall to her own room.

Leigh heard her drop the packages on her bed. Leigh got up and followed her.

"Aunt Florence, is the Souza—Oahu store around here somewhere?"

Florence stared across the room at her niece. An odd look crossed her face. "Wherever did you get that name?"

"From the back of the pendant you gave me. Here." Leigh crossed the room and showed her aunt. "Don't you remember? I showed it to you when we first got to Hawaii."

"Now, Leigh, I don't see how you can expect me to remember such a small detail—"

"Oh, for heaven's sake, Aunt Florence! Can't you remember anything for longer than three days?"

"You don't have to shout—"

"I'm sorry, but you're so frustrating sometimes!"

A new light entered the older woman's eyes. The vague pleasantness was gone. She looked shrewd and more lucid than Leigh had ever seen her.

"My forgetfulness frustrates you, doesn't it? In the twenty-six years you've known me, has it ever occurred to you that if I don't remember, it may be because I choose not to?"

A cold clamminess crawled up Leigh's back. The woman in front of her did not seem to be her aunt. Leigh had never seen that look in Florence's eyes.

She began in a low voice, "Please. This is very important to me. Can you remember where you got this?" She held out the pendant.

Florence stared at it. The shrewdness in her face disintegrated into confusion tinged with fear. She reached out trembling fingertips to touch the dully gleaming stone. "I think . . . from a stream. . . ."

Suddenly her hands went to her forehead. She closed her eyes and pressed the heels of her hands against her temples. "Oh!" she screamed. She stumbled over some of her shopping packages on her way to the bed. Leigh ran to her and grabbed her arm. She helped her lie down on the bed.

"My head, my head! It's split open!"

For a panicky moment Leigh took her literally and looked for blood. Then she realized her aunt must be talking about a headache. Leigh looked around the room and spotted Florence's makeup case. She went to it and rummaged through it until she found the bottle of Excedrin. Florence cried out and rolled over on the bed, still clutching her head. Leigh ran into the bathroom for a glass of water. She returned to Florence's bedside and pulled her up to a sitting position.

"Here, take these!" Leigh pushed the caplets into her mouth and put the glass of water to her lips. Florence grabbed the glass and gulped down the water. Then she fell back on the bed. In a moment she was asleep.

Leigh gazed down at her aunt. Her heart pounded in her ears. She held up the olivine pendant. It had caused her nothing but trouble since she got to Hawaii.

Florence stirred. Leigh glanced at her. She was awake. She smiled.

"I love you, Leigh. You're the child I never had." She wrapped her hand around Leigh's, the one that held the olivine pendant. She looked at it. ''Oh, what's this? The necklace you're going to wear to dinner tonight? Where would you like to go? I hear Don the Beachcomber's is very nice. . . .''

## Chapter Ten

Plagued by dreams, Leigh slept fitfully that night. She dreamed that Malcolm broke into their hotel room and found the olivine pendant. She tried to take it away from him but he pushed her back, back, back, until she was on the balcony. The railing was gone. The building began to sway and Aunt Florence screamed, clutching her head. She shouted to Leigh to watch out for the crouching lion. Leigh looked over her shoulder, lost her balance, and fell off the balcony. She fell slowly, slowly, and down below her she saw Kalani with his arms outstretched to catch her. Then, from above, she heard the beat-beat-beat of a helicopter and saw Malcolm signal Kalani not to catch her. He held up the olivine pendant. Kalani dropped his arms. . . .

Leigh sat up straight in bed, gasping for air. Gradually her breathing slowed to normal. She could see the first gray light of day outside the window. And down the hall she could see lamplight coming from her aunt's bedroom.

Leigh got out of bed and went down the hall to

Florence's room. She was in bed, asleep, a newspaper spread across her chest. The bedside lamp was on.

Leigh smiled fondly and went into the room. She lifted the newspaper off her aunt's chest. It was an old one from the stack Florence had found in the closet at the bungalow. On the front page was a picture of the girl who had been crowned Miss Hawaii that year. She wondered why Florence had brought this newspaper with her.

She folded the paper and laid it on the nightstand. In the harsh light of the bedside lamp Florence's sleeping face looked lined and drawn, as if in grief. She flicked off the light.

Florence stirred. She opened her eyes and looked around.

"Oh, good morning, Leigh."

"'Morning. I didn't mean to bother you. You slept with your light on all night. Fell asleep reading, I guess."

"What time is it?"

"About six. Go back to sleep."

"No, I'm ready to get up. We wanted to get an early start on the day, didn't we? Let's go."

After breakfast they decided to drive around the island to the north shore, where Waimea Falls Park was located. Florence threaded the car through the traffic of Waikiki toward the highway that belted the eastern curve of Oahu.

Honolulu receded behind them and they passed through green fields, thick stands of trees, now and then a house or a cluster of little stores by the roadside.

The warm breeze streamed in through the open car windows.

They passed a road sign that announced the town just ahead. Florence glanced at it and frowned. "Wasn't that the town they mentioned on the news last night? Where the rain is causing all those mudslides and those poor people are afraid of losing their homes?"

"Oh. I don't know. I can't remember." Leigh suddenly sat up straight and pointed out the window. "Look over there! That tiny green island in the ocean. It's shaped like a little green volcano, isn't it?"

Florence took her eyes from the road long enough to glance toward the small outcropping of rock just off the coast. The car swerved slightly. Leigh opened the road map on her lap.

"Let's see if it's on here. We just passed that little town, so it must be up here. . . . Yes, here it is! Perfect name for it. Guess what it's called? 'Chinaman's Hat.'"

The car swerved off the road and bumped violently across a rocky field before Florence brought it to a halt. For a moment Leigh sat stunned, clutching the dashboard. When she caught her breath, she turned to see if her aunt was all right.

Florence's grip on the steering wheel was so tight her knuckles showed white through the skin of her hands. Her blue-green eyes were wide and staring, reflecting the colors of the sky and the tiny cone-shaped island off the coast. Without moving her head she opened the door of the car.

"Aunt Florence?"

She did not answer. She got out of the car and stood, staring, at Chinaman's Hat. The tradewinds fluttered her light cotton skirt and lifted her hair. As Leigh watched, her shoulders straightened, her back arched, and she suddenly looked much younger. Even the way she lifted both hands to shield her eyes from the sun was the gesture of a young woman.

She turned and called cheerfully to Leigh, "Come here and look! It's just the way I remember it!"

Puzzled, Leigh climbed out of the car and walked over to her aunt. Florence looked off toward the north. "And that means the house must be farther on that way. We're almost there!"

"What house?"

"Our house." Florence grew serious. She leaned toward Leigh with a confidential air. "I'm going to tell you something. But you have to promise you won't tell your father."

Leigh felt a flash of uneasiness. "What is it?"

"We're married. No one's supposed to know for a while, especially your father, until we get some legal things settled."

"Married!" Leigh stepped back and gaped at her aunt. Simon and Florence were married! So that's why they had been spending so much time together. It had probably happened that night they went to Hilo. For the "fund-raiser." "Why didn't you tell me?"

"It was a secret ceremony. There was no other way. Please don't be hurt. You know I would have invited you if I could."

Leigh was speechless. She gazed out at Chinaman's Hat, then up the coast in the direction Florence had indicated. "And I suppose he has a house over there too."

"Yes."

"Does he have a house on every island?"

"No, just here and the Big Island. But he says he wants to live here. The other one is just too big and formal for him. That one will go to our children someday."

"Children! You're planning to have children?"

"Of course! In fact, I think I may already be pregnant."

"What!"

"Yes. Oh, Sharon, I'm so happy!"

Utter silence followed, unbroken except for the swish of the palm trees in the breeze and the distant rumble of the surf. Slowly, Leigh realized what she should have known since the beginning of the conversation. This was not Aunt Florence who was speaking—at least not the Aunt Florence she knew. This woman was probably twenty-five or thirty years younger, and she thought Leigh was her friend Sharon.

Had Florence been married to Simon thirty years ago? What had happened? Why could she remember none of this except during one of her ever more frequent spells?

Leigh grabbed the older woman's shoulders. "I'm not Sharon. Look at me. I'm Leigh Christie, your niece."

Florence stared at her. Slowly, her eyes seemed to focus. She looked around. "Why did we stop? Where are we?"

"You wanted to stop to see Chinaman's Hat, remember?"

"I thought we were going to Waimea Falls."

"We are. Let's get back in the car." In spite of the warm breeze and the golden sunlight spilling around her, a cold shudder went through Leigh. *I can't handle this,* she thought.

They got back into the car and slammed their doors. Florence reached for the keys in the ignition. Quickly, Leigh spoke.

"Did you get married the first time you were in Hawaii?"

"No, dear, I didn't get married until a few years later."

Leigh took a breath. "Were you ever married to Simon?"

Florence flushed a deep pink. She looked down at her lap. When she looked up again, she smiled shyly. "How did you find out that he's asked me to marry him?"

Leigh opened her mouth and then closed it. She was now thoroughly confused. "What? I mean, when did he ask you?"

"The night before we left the Big Island. At the charity dinner in Hilo. It was lovely."

"Well, what did you say?"

"I said I'd think about it while I was here. He said he'll have a diamond ring for me when I get back to help make up my mind."

Leigh's head was beginning to spin. "You still haven't answered my question. Were you married to Simon thirty years ago?"

"Of course not. Why would you ask a thing like that?"

"Because a little while ago you were—reminiscing. You said you were secretly married and you were going to live in a house he had not far from here. You said he didn't want to live in the house on the Big Island because it was too formal. You even said you thought you might be—pregnant."

Suddenly Florence cried out and pressed the palms of her hands to her temples. Leigh grabbed for her.

Florence shouted in obvious pain and rocked back and forth. Panicked, Leigh looked around for some help. They were alone out here except for the cars zooming by on the highway. Her aunt screamed and collapsed over the steering wheel.

Leigh got out of the car and went around to the driver's side. She opened the door and managed to push Florence over to the passenger side. She slid in behind the wheel and started the motor. With a crunch of tires over gravel she pulled the car out onto the highway and headed back toward Honolulu.

Tomorrow. If she could hang on until tomorrow she would be all right. She would be meeting her father for lunch at the Ala Moana Center. The thought flooded her with relief. Maybe he would know what was wrong with Florence.

The older woman stirred in the seat beside her. After a moment she sat up and looked around, blinking slowly.

"Isn't this the same little town we passed through a little while ago? The one with the mudslides. Oh, dear, if the rain's been this bad here it must have been worse on the Big Island. I hope Simon's all right. I hope I won't have to dig him out of the mud when I get back tomorrow. . . .''

For fear of bringing on another headache attack, Leigh said nothing more to her aunt about her apparent regressions into the past. When she had regained her mental equilibrium, Florence asked why they had not gone to Waimea Falls. Leigh said she wasn't feeling well and would rather spend the day lying out on the beach. Florence seemed almost relieved. When they got to the hotel room, she took a nap.

Leigh was convinced that Florence's spells were more than just fantasy. Something had happened thirty years ago here in Hawaii that had changed her aunt's life. And somehow Simon was involved.

Had she been married to Simon thirty years ago? If so, why had they parted? And why had Simon never acknowledged their relationship? Why would he want to marry her again?

Because this wasn't Simon. The real Simon was dead. Leigh had seen his grave.

Something Kalani had said popped into her mind. *They became best friends. . . . Uncle Moe never got married, and Simon was married only once for a couple of years. . . .*

A couple of years. Had Florence been in Hawaii that long the first time? Leigh's father would know. He might know a lot of things. She could hardly wait to see him.

Florence was already dressed by the time Leigh got up the next morning. Leigh could sense her aunt's excitement. *She's eager to get back to Simon,* she thought. *Whoever he really is, Florence has fallen in love with him.*

They drove to the airport and Leigh parked the car. She accompanied her aunt into the terminal, where Florence checked her bags and then looked at her watch. "Well, I suppose you should be heading for the Delta terminal soon to pick up your father." She smiled and patted Leigh's cheek. Her hand carried the subtle scent of the expensive perfume she wore. "I'll miss you till tomorrow, Leigh—mess and all."

"Aunt Florence, are you going to accept Simon's marriage proposal?"

For an instant she looked startled. Then she relaxed. "Oh, that's right, I did tell you about that, didn't I? Yes, Leigh, I think I will. We'll probably announce it at the party tonight."

"Don't you think you should think it over a little longer before you give him an answer?"

Florence gave a little smile. There was a glint in her eye—the same shrewd, hard look that had frightened Leigh in the hotel room three days ago—and then it was gone. "No, dear. It may seem that Simon and I have only been interested in each other the past week or so, but that's not quite true. We've known each other for years. There's always been a particular bond between Simon and me. Besides, I'm fifty years old and not getting any younger. It'll be nice to be married again. Nice to live in Hawaii again. Oh, there's the call for my flight. See you tomorrow." Florence smiled and waved and hurried in the direction of the boarding gate.

Leigh merely stared after her. Nice to live in Hawaii *again.*

When Leigh spotted her father striding across the Delta terminal, her heart leaped with happiness. She had always been close to her father and was especially glad to see him now, when there were so many perplexing questions to be answered.

Her father was six feet one, lanky, well-dressed, his brown hair touched with gray at the temples. Like Leigh's, his eyes were greenish-blue behind his glasses. His attractive face broke into a smile when he saw her. Leigh ran into his outstretched arms.

"Hi, honey! Does this mean you're glad to see your old man?"

"Nah. I always run into the arms of handsome men." She smiled and kissed his cheek.

"Where's Florence? I'm expecting another big reception."

"Sorry to disappoint you, Dad, but Aunt Florence just lifted off the runway. She's going back to the Big Island today. Simon promised to throw her a party tonight. She didn't want to miss it." Leigh wanted to ask him how much he knew about Simon, but decided to wait until they got to Ala Moana.

She linked her hand through his elbow. "Come on. The car's waiting outside."

The restaurant atop the Ala Moana Center offered a spectacular view of Waikiki and most of Honolulu. Leigh and her father were seated at a window table, and they gazed through the smoked glass toward the sweeping thrust of Diamond Head as they ate.

They were almost finished with lunch before Leigh decided to plunge into her questions.

"Dad, how old was Aunt Florence the first time she visited Hawaii?"

"About twenty-two, I guess. She was almost twenty-four when she came home."

"So it was more than a visit."

"Turned out that way. She came out on one of those college tours that was supposed to last four weeks, and wound up staying about a year and a half. Our parents weren't too happy about it, either. But what could they do? She was a big girl."

"Dad, why doesn't she remember any of that?"

Grant Christie wiped his mouth with the linen napkin and laid it down beside his empty plate. He aligned the silverware on the tablecloth and looked out the window toward Diamond Head. Leigh waited. Finally he answered.

"Just before Florence left Hawaii she was in a bad bus accident just outside of Hilo. A lot of people were killed. Florence got a nasty head wound. She lost part of her memory and she's never regained it. She has no recollection of the accident or of the year and a half she spent in Hawaii. The only reason we know of the accident is because the Hawaiian authorities notified us."

Bus accident. The newspaper article. "Was anyone with her on the bus?"

He shook his head. "No. And after she came home, no one she had known in Hawaii contacted her."

"Except Simon."

"No, she met Simon through Ross."

Leigh no longer believed that, but she did not say as much. "Did she get married during the year and a half she lived here?"

Her father looked somewhat astonished. "Why, no. At least, not as far as I know. I'm sure she would have told us at the time. All her identification said Florence Christie. No name change."

*It was a secret ceremony. There was no other way. . . . But you have to promise not to tell your father.*

"Leigh." Her father's tone was serious. "Has something happened? How is Florence?"

"Dad, has Aunt Florence ever been to a doctor for her amnesia?"

It was as if she had finally asked the dreaded question. Her father sank back in his chair. "Yes. The doctor told us that for some reason her mind refuses to remember anything that had happened. He said that if we forced it, she could have violent headaches and her behavior would be unpredictable, possibly dangerous. He said that when her mind was ready to handle it, the memory would return. So far it hasn't. That was almost twenty-six years ago." There was a pause. "Has she begun to remember?"

"A little. But most of it's been forced, I think. Things and places and people bring back the memories. She's had those violent headaches you talked about."

"I should have explained all this to you ahead of time. This has always been one of those family secrets no one wants to talk about. You weren't even born when it happened, and by the time you were old enough to understand, it had just become a part of life."

A thought came to Leigh. She opened her purse and took out the olivine pendant.

"Do you recognize this?"

He looked at it for a few seconds and nodded. "That was with Florence's things when she came back from Hawaii with amnesia. I never saw her wear it after she married Ross. Where did you get it?"

"Aunt Florence gave it to me. Do you know where she got it?"

"Somewhere in Hawaii. Have you seen many of them around?"

"Only one other. It belongs to a man named Kalani Akina. He lives on the Big Island."

"Is he Florence's age?"

"Oh, no. He's only a couple years older than I am."

"Maybe he inherited it, the way you did. Listen, sweetheart, I think you'd better come home. Maybe Florence's return to Hawaii will prove to be good therapy for her, but I don't think you can handle her on your own."

"But we still have two weeks left! It'll be all right, Dad. Now that I know what's going on, I'll avoid bringing anything up that might get her started. And she isn't dangerous. She just has splitting headaches. . . ." Leigh trailed off. She suddenly remembered Florence's words during her first violent headache in Honolulu. *My head! It's split open!* Now Leigh understood. She had been reliving the bus accident.

"I'll tell you what," her father said with an air of reluctant compromise, "I'm going to be in Tokyo for three days. Then I'll fly back here and join you on the

Big Island. If she's had any more spells, you're both flying back to L.A. with me. Deal?''

"Deal."

He looked at his watch. "We should be getting back to the airport. My plane leaves in an hour. Ready, driver?''

Leigh drove her father back to the airport and saw him off. Then she drove back toward her hotel and Waikiki Beach.

But when she got into the congested traffic of Waikiki, she realized she could not spend her last afternoon on the beach. There was one more place she had to try to find before she left Oahu.

And so she drove back onto the highway she and Florence had taken the day before.

Chinaman's Hat came into view off the coast. Leigh did not pull off the road where Florence had the day before, but continued along the highway toward the north shore of the island. Florence had looked that direction when she said, *The house must be farther on that way. We're almost there.*

The house. Had she and Simon lived there as newlyweds thirty years ago? How was Leigh going to find it? She had to try.

She drove on for several miles, reading every sign she passed, watching for a house that might give her some clue by its appearance.

And then she saw it. A sign outside a restaurant. Leigh pulled off the road and climbed out of the car. For several minutes she simply stared across the two-lane highway, shielding her eyes against the sun.

The Crouching Lion Restaurant.

It was late afternoon and the shadows stretched across the highway. The sun was setting behind the shoulder of the Crouching Lion and, looking around, Leigh could see a small souvenir shop and the dirt parking lot where her car was parked.

The sign over the door of the shop caught her eye. At first she thought she had read it wrong and she walked closer for a better look. But she had read it correctly.

*Souza—Oahu.*

## Chapter Eleven

The breeze came up and swayed the shingle over the door. Souza—Oahu. Leigh went up the wooden steps to the screen door and pulled it open.

The small shop was crowded with an array of goods that appealed to vacationers. A Coke machine stood to the right of the door; to the left was a long glass display case. In the case were chunks of lace coral on three-legged wooden stands; gold-dipped maile leaves on fine chains; and gold and silver jewelry set with coral and mother-of-pearl. And olivine.

A short, sturdily built man in his late sixties sat on a stool behind the counter next to the cash register. He had the olive skin and dark eyes of southern Europe; his thick hair and eyebrows were pure white. He looked up as the screen door opened. When he saw Leigh he smiled, a twinkle in his eye.

"Aloha," he greeted as Leigh approached. "How are you today?"

"Hopeful," she replied honestly. "I hope you can help me."

"So do I. Helping lovely young ladies is my favorite hobby."

"Don't mind him. He's been a flirt since before I married him."

Leigh turned and looked toward the back of the shop. A short, round, gray-haired woman in a muumuu and zoris was flipping a feather duster over the back shelves. She gave Leigh a friendly smile.

Leigh smiled too. "Are you Mr. Souza?"

"Yes, I am. How can I help you?"

Leigh took the olivine pendant out of her purse. "Do you recognize this?"

Mr. Souza looked at it. He took it out of Leigh's hand and turned it over. Suddenly his face broke into an astonished smile.

"I don't believe it. Fatima! Come here, I want to show you."

The woman came out from behind the shelves. "What is it now?" she asked with teasing exasperation. She peered over her husband's shoulder at the piece of jewelry in his hand.

"Do you recognize it?"

"Yes!" she said. "My goodness, that must have been twenty-five, twenty-six years ago, but you don't forget something like that. They were such a nice couple. The baby must be all grown up by now."

"Who are you talking about?" Leigh asked urgently.

"The people I made this for," Mr. Souza said. "They came in one day with a big rock of olivine. They had found it in a stream when they were on a picnic and they wanted matching pendants made from it. So I made three pendants—one for the husband, one for the wife, one for the baby."

The baby. *I think I may already be pregnant.* ''Was the man much older than the woman?'' Leigh asked.

''Oh, yes. She was in her early twenties—pretty little thing, big blue eyes like yours—and he was past forty. He looked younger, but Hawaiians hold their age well.''

It took Leigh a moment to absorb what he had just said. ''The man was Hawaiian?''

''Yes, I remember that,'' Mrs. Souza said. ''I asked them how they met. I guess I'm pretty nosy, but I think it's fun to find out about people. He was a university professor and she was a visiting college student. Oh, they loved each other so much. Remember, Eduardo? The way they cuddled and kissed that little baby.''

''The piece of olivine they gave me wasn't very pretty—well, you can see for yourself. The kind of olivine we use in jewelry is usually this color.'' He pointed through the glass of the display case at a lime-colored ring. ''But this piece of olivine meant more to them. They had found it together and they would wear it together. The whole family. They came back a week or so later and I had all three pendants finished. The mother held the baby while the father put one of the pendants over its little head. The chain was a little too long. But I'm sure it isn't now.''

Mrs. Souza was watching Leigh. ''Is this pendant yours, honey?''

Leigh took it back from Mr. Souza. ''No. It's my aunt's.''

''She was the blue-eyed young girl?''

Leigh nodded.

''And her husband?''

"My aunt is a widow."

"Oh. We're so sorry."

Before they could ask the next question, Leigh lifted her head brusquely and smiled. "Thank you very much for helping me. I—" But she could not finish. Quickly she turned and left the store.

Leigh got into the car and started the motor. As she guided the car onto the highway toward Honolulu, snatches of remembered conversation came to her. Kalani's voice. *Uncle Moekane was a professor at the University of Hawaii on Oahu. . . . Uncle Moe never got married and Simon was married only once for a couple of years. . . . My mother was a* haole *girl. . . . Uncle Moe never got married. . . .*

Aunt Florence, girlish, conspiratorial: *We're married. No one's supposed to know for a while, especially your father, until we get some legal things settled. . . . It was a secret ceremony. There was no other way. . . .*

Mrs. Souza: *That must have been twenty-five, twenty-six years ago. . . . The way they cuddled and kissed that little baby. . . .*

Mr. Souza: *The chain was a little too long. But I'm sure it isn't now. . . .*

*No,* Leigh thought, *it isn't now. He wears it well.* Kalani was her cousin.

Leigh returned to the penthouse suite and pondered the situation in the lonely quiet.

The bus accident. Moe and Florence had been on that bus together. Moe had been killed and Florence had lost her memory. Her identification had never been changed: It still said Florence Christie, not Florence Akina.

Moe's body had been claimed by his family and Florence had been taken to the hospital. What about the baby? Was he with them on the bus? If his family knew nothing of the marriage, why would they accept Kalani as an Akina?

Perhaps Moekane's younger brother knew of the marriage. Perhaps he had been sworn to secrecy, and when Moekane died, he took the baby and adopted him as his own. Perhaps that was why Kalani had been told that a dead white woman was his mother. When, in fact, she was very much alive.

Leigh got up and went to the sliding glass door. She opened it and stepped out onto the balcony. Dusk had fallen, and lights were twinkling all over Waikiki. The air was heavy and moist, signaling an approaching storm. Below her in the International Marketplace, colored paper lanterns bobbed and swayed in the wind. Off to her right, down on Kalakaua Avenue, Leigh saw the store Yamashiro Ltd Honolulu.

How was Malcolm involved in all of this?

Leigh came awake abruptly in the middle of the night. For a minute she lay still, listening. The suite seemed eerie without Florence's presence in the next room.

She had the sensation of the building swaying. She shut her eyes and pulled up the covers around her chin. She heard the splatter of rain, hard and steady, on the balcony.

Something was bothering her. She sat up and tried to figure out what it was.

Simon. He and Moe Akina had been close friends. He must have known about Moe's marriage to Florence. Unless, of course, the marriage had been so private not even he was informed of it.

Maybe that was it. The friendship had disintegrated, probably before Moe and Florence were married. Yet the will had been left standing—not out of forgetfulness but because the marriage produced offspring that would, according to the will, inherit Moe's estate instead of Simon.

Simon would understandably have been resentful. Moe might have feared that, had Simon known about his wife and child, he would have done something drastic to get them out of the way.

But the bus accident solved all of Simon's problems. Moekane was killed, Florence forgot everything and left Hawaii, and Simon inherited the York estate.

Had someone killed Simon and taken on his identity?

The man who was living at Wailani was not safe. Florence's memory might come back. That was why he had traced her to California, made friends with her husband, kept in close contact all these years. He was afraid that someday she would remember.

What would he do when she did?

Leigh thought of her aunt's frightening spells, her dreams, her regressions into the past. Things were beginning to emerge. She was starting to remember.

Florence had flown back to the Big Island today for Simon's party. What if her memory clicked into place and it all came spilling out when she was alone with him? What would he do? What was he capable of?

Leigh threw back the covers and climbed out of bed. She could not sleep anymore. She wandered out of her bedroom and down the hall to the now-empty second bedroom. She leaned against the doorjamb and looked around the room.

The maid had been in yesterday to make the bed and straighten the room. Once again it looked impersonal, as if Aunt Florence had never been there.

Except for the newspaper. It was folded neatly on the nightstand, exactly as Florence had left it.

No, not exactly as she had left it. She crossed the room and picked up the paper. It was folded open to the second page. Leigh turned on the lamp. Near the bottom of the page a small item was circled in blue ink. The ink looked fresh against the yellowed newsprint.

> *An investigation is being conducted into the death of Moekane Akina, found dead at the scene of a bus accident last week. Authorities now suspect foul play in Akina's death, after discovering wounds on his head that appear to have been caused by repeated blows with a heavy object. A coroner's inquest is pending.*

Leigh stared at the circle of blue ink around the article. Florence had made it. Which meant that she must, by now, remember everything. . . . *I always felt there was some grand passion in my life that I had missed.*

Leigh ran to her room. She flipped on the light, saw it was five-thirty in the morning, and picked up the phone.

"Front desk."

"I'd like to make a call to the Big Island."

"Number, please?"

Leigh closed her eyes and tried to gather her thoughts. There was no telephone at the bungalow. Whom should she call? Simon? The man she suspected of killing Florence's husband?

No. There was someone else, someone more personally involved. It was only fitting to call him. It seemed the right thing to do.

"Miss, are you still there?"

"Yes. I need to make a call to Honola'i on the Big Island. I don't have the number. The name is Akina."

"One moment." There was a long pause, then Leigh heard the number being dialed. One ring. Another.

"Hello?" a low, sleepy voice said.

"Kalani? It's Leigh."

"Leigh!" His voice suddenly sounded wide awake.

"Yes. I'm sorry to call you so early but—"

"Never mind. Where are you?"

"At my hotel in Honolulu. I need to talk to my aunt, but there's no phone at the bungalow. Would you please give her a message for me as soon as possible? It's urgent."

"Of course." His voice was calm, decisive. She heard a rustle of paper. "What is it?"

"Tell her to stay away from Simon. Tell her not to say anything to him until I get back."

"Simon? Why? You sound like you're afraid of him."

Leigh hesitated. "I am. And you should be too."

There was a long silence. Finally Kalani said, "So you know."

This caught Leigh by surprise. For a moment she was speechless. "What?"

"How did you find out?"

"Kalani. . . . You mean you've known all along? Why didn't you say anything?"

"Reasons of my own. Look, I'll take your message to Florence and we'll come to the airport for you. When does your plane come in?"

"Ten o'clock this morning."

"Okay. We'll see you at ten." There was a click and then the dial tone.

Slowly, Leigh replaced the receiver. For a long time she stared at the telephone. She did not feel as relieved as she thought she should.

Kalani was waiting for her at the airport when she got off the plane in Hilo. She spotted him in the crowd at the arrival gate. She didn't see Florence.

He came forward to meet her. Her heart surged with happiness at the sight of him—in spite of his blood relationship to her. At that moment Leigh knew that she loved him. It was one of the great ironies of her life that the one man she had ever loved was the one man she couldn't have.

He took her elbow and steered her toward the baggage claim area. His touch made her as giddy as a schoolgirl and she pulled her arm out of his grasp. For the sake of her sanity, she realized she would have to leave Hawaii as soon as possible.

Kalani gave her a puzzled look. "Is something wrong?"

"No. Yes—but only with me. Never mind." She looked around. "Where's Aunt Florence?"

"I don't know."

"What do you mean, you don't—"

"She wasn't at the bungalow. When no one answered my knock, I went in and looked around. All her things are there—her clothes, even her suitcase—so wherever she went, she didn't expect to be gone for long."

"She went to Simon's party last night. Maybe she stayed—"

"I already checked with Derek. He said he hadn't seen her since the party last night. I asked him to check all the bedrooms and he did. She wasn't there. So I called the police."

Leigh glanced up at him as they hurried along. "And?"

"And they said they couldn't list her as a missing person until she'd been gone for twenty-four hours."

"Where's Simon?"

"Derek doesn't know. He isn't at Wailani. He left late last night and hasn't come back."

They retrieved Leigh's luggage at the baggage claim area and left the terminal. The morning was dark and moist with the last of the tropical storm. "Over here," Kalani said, and led her across the parking lot to his Bronco.

They drove away from the airport and sped north on

the highway. Kalani was strangely silent. Leigh studied him quietly—the long legs, the brown hands on the steering wheel, the rather royal profile. Her cousin—and he had known all along. She remembered what he had said on the veranda, two days after he had kissed her. *I should never have kissed you. . . . But not for the reason you think.*

"How long have you known?" she finally asked.

He flicked a glance toward her. "Since I was a little boy. My father thought I should know. How did you find out?"

"A lot of little pieces finally fell into place. But this was the key to it all." She took the olivine pendant out of her purse and let it dangle by its chain. "Do you recognize this?"

Kalani's hand went to his neck. "How did you get that?" he demanded.

"It's my aunt's. She got it the first time she was in Hawaii. Don't worry, I didn't steal yours. I thought you had stolen mine when I saw you wearing it at the party the other night. I was mad at you for days until I found it. Where did you get yours?"

"It was my uncle Moe's. After the accident they sent all his personal belongings to my father. That pendant was one of them. When I was about fifteen, I decided I liked it, so my father let me have it."

Leigh blinked. This possibility had not occurred to her. "Are you sure?"

"Yeah. What's the matter?"

"I—I don't know. Look. See what it says on the back? 'Souza—Oahu.' Does yours say that?"

"Yes."

"Well, I found Mr. Souza yesterday. He remembers making these for a married couple over twenty-five years ago. He was a forty-year-old university professor, a Hawaiian. She was a *haole* girl in her early twenties. Mr. Souza made three pendants, one for each of them and one for the baby."

Kalani stared at the road, then he shot her a suspicious look. "Are you trying to tell me my uncle was married to your aunt? That's impossible. He was never married. My father would have known."

"It was a secret ceremony. They didn't want anyone to know they were married. I think they didn't want Simon to know. He had the most to lose, especially if they had a baby. Isn't that what your uncle Moe's will said?"

Kalani nodded wordlessly. He was obviously overwhelmed.

"Why is this such a shock to you? Just ten minutes ago you said you've known since you were a little boy—"

"I had no idea. I thought you were talking about something else. I never knew about this." He glanced at her. "Does Simon know?"

"I'm sure he does by now. Your uncle must have known that he would kill to get Wailani. He was right, unfortunately."

"What do you mean?"

Leigh jumped. Kalani had an awful look on his face.

"Tell me! What have you found out?"

"I—I found an old newspaper my aunt left behind. It came out about a week after the bus crash. An article in it said that the accident didn't kill your uncle. There was evidence that somebody may have murdered him.''

They drove in silence for several miles. Leigh watched Kalani. He looked straight ahead, a stony set to his jaw, his large hands gripping the steering wheel.

''You don't believe me, do you?''

''Yes, I do. I believe everything you've said.'' Kalani took a slow, careful breath. ''My father told me about my uncle's death. He said that the authorities suspected that Moe might have been murdered because of the nature of his wounds. But they could never find a suspect or a motive, and so the case was closed. For years my father suspected Simon, but he could never prove anything. And, of course, he didn't know about Uncle Moe's marriage.''

''Well, Aunt Florence is off alone somewhere with Simon. I'm sure her memory's come back by now and I'm sure he knows it. If Simon killed once to get Wailani, he'll kill again to keep it!''

''I'll take you back to the bungalow and then take my boat out to look for them along the coast. It hasn't rained since yesterday and the ocean isn't quite as rough. And I'll call the police again. Maybe they'll listen this time.''

''Thank you.'' She regarded Kalani's set profile for a moment. ''You're afraid of Simon too, aren't you?''

He nodded slowly. ''I've always been afraid of him. Sometimes I'm surprised he hasn't tried to kill me.''

Leigh threw him a look. *So now he knows,* she thought. *He's figured out who the baby was.* ''Why would he want to kill you?'' she asked carefully.

"Because he believes I'm responsible for the death of his daughter."

Leigh wasn't sure she had heard him right. "His daughter!"

Kalani nodded. "He was married once, remember? Just long enough to produce a child. He was crazy about her. When she was older, he got custody of her. She was the only person on earth he loved."

*Please don't tell me she died of a drug overdose,* Leigh pleaded silently. But she had to know.

"Why does he hold you responsible?"

"Because she died giving birth to me. Sharon Trowbridge was my mother."

For a long time Leigh could not speak. Sharon Trowbridge. . . . *Oh, Sharon, I'm so happy! No one's supposed to know for a while, especially your father.*

Leigh shook her head to clear it. "You mean, Simon's your grandfather?"

"Yeah. Funny, huh?"

Leigh stared out the window. They were approaching the turnoff for Honola'i. To their right the land fell away to the crashing surf below.

*My mother was a* haole *girl.* Sharon Trowbridge was Kalani's mother, not Florence Christie. Kalani was not Leigh's cousin after all.

Relief rushed over Leigh and made her light-headed. She began to laugh. Kalani gave her a strange look.

"What's so funny?"

"I thought the *haole* girl who was your mother was my aunt Florence. I thought you were my cousin."

Kalani stared at her. Then, remembering what he

was doing, he glanced back at the road. "Your cousin!"

"Yes. There wasn't a doubt in my mind. It was terribly depressing." She studied his face. She could see the resemblance now: He had Simon's aquiline nose, his square jaw, his height. "So you never knew your mother."

"No."

"How did she and your father meet?"

"My father took care of the estate for Uncle Moe, but Simon used to visit a lot. Uncle Moe gave him free run of the place. He brought his daughter with him sometimes. That's how Sharon and my father met. Simon had no idea they were involved until he found out my mother was pregnant. That's when he cut off all contact with our family. He wouldn't let my mother see my father again, nor would he talk to Uncle Moe. That's what ended their friendship.

"My mother was nineteen when I was born. There were complications, I guess, and she died. Simon was crazy with grief. He delivered me to my father and said he did not want to be known as my grandfather, didn't want to be connected with the Akinas in any way. My father respected his wishes. Very few people know I'm Simon's grandson. When I was five, Pop married my stepmother. She's the only mother I've known.

"Simon loved my mother more than anything in the world. Her death almost destroyed him. After he inherited Wailani, he had her body moved to the family plot there."

Leigh's mouth fell open. "S. Trowbridge. Of course."

"What?"

"I saw her grave. I thought it was. . . ." She frowned. "I saw an older, well-dressed woman. She was walking away from the grave when I saw her. She left a bouquet of anthurium—"

"That was my grandmother. Simon's ex-wife, Laura. She was on the Big Island a few days ago."

"Are you in contact with her?"

"Yes. She visits every once in a while. She doesn't blame us for what happened."

For a long time they drove in silence. As they turned down onto the Honola'i road, Leigh spoke.

"My aunt Florence knew Sharon. They were friends. Your mother knew that Florence and Moe were married."

Kalani frowned with thought. "You said Uncle Moe and Florence had a baby. What happened to it?"

There was a long silence. "I don't know," Leigh said.

They pulled up in front of the bungalow. A light mist had begun to fall. Water dripped from the leaves of the plumeria tree; the ground was soggy and deep red. Kalani took Leigh's bags out of the back of the Bronco and followed her up to the front door.

Leigh had hoped that somehow Florence would be there when she opened the door, fussing about the mess in her room. But only silence greeted her. They went inside, but her search through the bungalow produced no clues.

"I'll take the boat out and look," Kalani said. "You

stay here. Don't open the door to anyone except your aunt.'' He turned to give her a half smile. He stopped. The quiet fire in his eyes drained the strength from Leigh. *Come to me, enfold me in your arms, let me feel your hand beneath my neck. . . .*

But he did not come to her. Something Leigh could not understand still held him back. He went out the door and closed it behind him.

Leigh closed her eyes and heaved a long sigh. She watched him through the window as he climbed into the Bronco and drove away. Simon's grandson.

Something worrisome nagged at the back of her mind. Malcolm. The marijuana house. Kalani's involvement in all of it. When she thought Kalani was Florence's son she had immediately set aside all her fears and suspicions. Now they returned, still unresolved. And now she knew that he was Simon's grandson. Simon, who may have killed to get Wailani. Did he really hate his grandson, his only flesh and blood? Or did Kalani tell her that to cover up deeper motives?

*Aunt Florence, where are you?*

Leigh wandered distractedly into her aunt's bedroom. The room looked different, somehow, and after a minute Leigh realized why. It was not quite tidy. Newspapers were scattered on the bed and the closet door was open. This would not have bothered Leigh in her own room, but in her aunt's room it looked uncomfortable, unnatural.

Leigh pulled the olivine pendant out of her purse. She laid it down on the nightstand and picked up one of the newspapers from the bed. It was the old newspaper with the article about the bus accident. She read it through again. A line jumped out at her: *Eleven people were killed, among them an unidentified baby girl between four and six months of age.*

A baby girl. Leigh lowered the paper and stared at the wall, trying to remember what the Souzas had said. They had never actually mentioned the sex of the baby.

A wave of sadness swept over Leigh. Her baby cousin had died. It would be difficult for Aunt Florence when she finally remembered. She had always wanted a daughter.

Leigh heard a vehicle pull up outside. She ran to the window and peeked out through the shutters. It was George's Jeep. Relief swept through her as she saw him get out.

A moment later it was squelched. Simon climbed out of the passenger side of the Jeep.

Leigh ducked away from the window. Panicked, she looked around the room. She ran into the closet and pulled the door closed. She backed into the corner, behind her aunt's dresses, and knelt down.

The front doorknob rattled. A moment later there was the scrape of a key in the lock.

She could hear their voices, anxious and hostile, in the front room. The voices came closer. Leigh's blood pounded in her ears. She pressed her hands against the back of the closet. The painted wall had a slightly rough texture under her fingers. The clothes in front of her face smelled faintly of her aunt's perfume.

Simon and George were in the bedroom now.

"She's not here." George's voice.

"She couldn't have just vanished!"

"You say the last time you saw her was at the party last night? Were any cars missing?"

"No." Simon sounded agitated. "It was right after she refused my ring. She said there was something she wanted to talk to me about. She was upset. I hope she didn't do something foolish. I wonder if Leigh figured out what's going on and told her about it."

"I don't think so. Leigh still believes what we wanted her to believe. It pays to have her confidence. She's the one who told me Malcolm knew about our drop on Saturday. It gave me enough time to switch it to tonight."

A lance of disappointment stabbed through her fear. *Oh, George,* she thought. *I believed we were friends.*

"I'm surprised she hasn't reported Akina to the police," he said.

A laugh from Simon. "She would have held off anyway."

"What do you mean?"

"I mean, my young friend, that she's fallen for him. . . . Wait. Didn't I see some luggage out there? Isn't she supposed to be back today?"

There was a pause. "She was supposed to call me when she was ready to be picked up. I haven't heard anything."

"But if her luggage is out there. . . ." Simon's voice grew quiet. "Maybe she's figured things out and she's hiding from us. Check the closet."

*No,* Leigh prayed, *not in here, don't look in here, please. . . .*

The closet door opened. She held her breath, ex-

pecting any moment that the clothes in front of her
would be pushed aside.

"Wait a minute." Simon's voice came from over
near the bed.

"What?" Leigh could see George's feet below the
hanging dresses.

"Look at this."

George moved away from the closet. The door was
still open. Leigh moved her head slightly. She could
see Simon standing near the bed. He had picked up
the olivine pendant. He and George both looked at it
and then at each other.

"Have you seen that necklace of corals?" Simon
asked. "I saw it on her at the party last night. Do you
know what this means?"

George nodded. "I know where she is," he said.

"So do I. Let's go."

Abruptly, they left. A moment later Leigh heard the
Jeep drive away.

She crawled out of the closet and straightened up.
Her heart was still pounding painfully. She looked
around for the olivine pendant and could not find it.
Simon had taken it with him.

The necklace of corals. Aunt Florence had planned
to wear it to the party last night. She had bought it at
Malcolm's father's store.

Leigh went to the window and looked out. Where
had they gone? Why did they suddenly know where
Florence was? She sank down on the bed. Where was
Aunt Florence? What significance did her coral necklace have?

And then it struck her.

Simon had not asked George if he had seen that necklace of corals.

He asked if he had seen that necklace of Coral's.

*Chapter Twelve*

The path to Coral's house was slippery with mud. Leigh hurried along it as best she could and finally arrived, cold and rain-soaked.

She pounded on the door. No one answered. She pounded again, desperately. After a moment she saw someone peek around the bamboo shade in the window. The door opened. Emma peered out at her.

"Ko'a not home!" she shouted over the patter of the rain.

"Where is she?"

"Don' know." The old woman looked sullen. Leigh wasn't sure if it was because she truly didn't know or because she didn't want to tell her. Leigh suspected Emma was jealous of her friendship with Coral.

"Please, I have to know. It's very important!"

Emma's expression changed. "How come? What's the matter?"

"My aunt is missing. I can't find her. Nobody can."

Emma's eyes narrowed. "What's that got to do wit' Ko'a?"

"Was Simon here a few minutes ago? With George Honua?"

156

"No. Why would they come here?"

"They're looking for Coral. At least I think they are. I'm not sure of anything anymore."

Emma watched her closely. She seemed to be turning things over in her mind. "Why they need to look for her? She's up at Mr. Trowbridge's house, cleaning up after the party."

The cold suddenly hit Leigh. She shivered. Emma's gruff facade cracked. She took Leigh's shoulder and pulled her into the house.

"Come inside. No use you freezin' to death."

Gratefully, Leigh entered the back door of the house and found herself in Emma's bedroom. The woman hurried away to the bathroom and returned with a towel, which she threw around Leigh's shoulders. She clutched the warm terry cloth close to her.

"Now what's this about yo' aunt missing?" Emma demanded. She was half a foot shorter than Leigh but her expression, as she looked up, allowed for no resistance.

"I don't know where she is," Leigh said. "She came back from Honolulu ahead of me and now I can't find her."

"You ask Mr. Trowbridge?"

"No. I'm afraid to."

"How come?"

Leigh looked at the old Hawaiian woman. "I just found out that my aunt was married to Moekane Akina." The shocked expression on Emma's face was rather gratifying. "She doesn't remember because she got amnesia in the bus accident that killed him. But I also found out that he was probably murdered. And

I'm sure Simon is the one who killed him, so he could have Wailani. Now I've found out Kalani is his grandson and he's probably helping him—'' Leigh's breath caught at the stab of pain that went through her.

"Didn't I tell you Kalani was no good? Now maybe you'll listen!"

Leigh went on, aware that she was jabbering but unable to stop herself. "Even George is working with Simon. They're after my aunt and if Simon finds her before I do, I'm afraid he'll kill her the way he killed Moe!"

Emma stared at her. Gradually a light dawned in her eyes. The pieces were coming together for her too.

"He took Ko'a!" she cried. "He better not do nothing to her!" She ran from the room. Leigh followed her down the hall to the kitchen. Emma picked up the telephone and dialed furiously.

"Hello! Derek? Is Mr. Trowbridge there? How 'bout Ko'a? Where did they go? You never know nothing! Come down here plenty quick! We got trouble." Emma slammed down the receiver and turned to Leigh. "He took my Ko'a somewhere! And I bet I know where they are."

"You do? Where?"

"Think about it. Criminals always return to the scene of the crime. I bet they're at the place where Trowbridge killed Moekane."

"You mean the place where the bus went off the road?"

"Of course! That's where they'd go. That's where he took my Ko'a."

"Let's go!" Leigh cried. "Can we take your car?"

"We're not driving. We take boat."

"Boat? But if they're on the highway where the bus accident was, wouldn't it be easier to get there by car?"

"No. Much faster by boat. Road goes like this." She traced a tortuous line in the air. "Boat goes this way." A straight line.

"But the weather's bad. Are you sure it'll be safe?"

"Derek knows how to handle a boat." She threw Leigh a challenging look. "You afraid?"

"Yes," she answered honestly. "But I'm going with you anyway." She had no intention of being left behind again today. "But once we get there, won't it be hard to get up to the highway from the beach? I mean, isn't it a cliff—"

Emma threw up her hands. "What is this, a pop quiz? Just never mind. You see. I gonna find my Ko'a." Emma looked down. *She loves that girl,* Leigh thought. *She's as worried as I am. But we'll find them. We've got to.*

Leigh helped Emma hitch the boat trailer to her dilapidated truck. They towed the boat down to the launch at the south end of the cove and pushed the boat off the trailer and onto the ramp. The rain had stopped, but the ocean was gray and choppy and slapped angrily against the ramp.

Derek came panting down to the boat launch from the road. He was still in his white houseboy's clothes and his black hair was wet and plastered to his forehead. When he reached the ramp, Emma grumbled something to him. He glanced past her at Leigh. He looked frightened. *He's afraid he's going to lose Coral again,* Leigh thought. She knew just how he felt.

Leigh and Emma climbed into the boat. Emma removed a spear gun from the seat and set it on the floor
of the boat. Derek shoved the boat into the water and
clambered aboard. The boat heaved and dipped in the
restless sea. Derek sat down at the tiller. A moment
later the motor sputtered to life. The boat shuddered
and groaned and slowly moved out of the cove into
the open sea.

The little boat gathered speed and the bow flung
saltwater spray into their faces as it cut through the
water. Leigh sat on her bench seat, clutching the sides,
and gazed straight ahead, her eyes squinted against the
salt spray. Now that she was actively involved in finding Florence she felt better. It wouldn't be long now.

She glanced at Emma. The tough old woman was
watching her. Her eyes were accusing.

*Does she blame me for the trouble Coral's in?* Leigh
wondered. *How can she? I had nothing to do with it.
I only overheard Simon, saw him pick up the olivine
pendant, and connected it with Coral's necklace. . . .*

Coral's necklace. She had been too preoccupied to
think about its significance until now. Did it look like
Florence's pendant? It must. Why else would Simon
have mentioned it? And if it looked like Florence's, it
must be . . . the third olivine pendant.

Moe's had gone to his nephew, Florence's had gone
to her niece. But the baby's had stayed with her. Coral
was Florence's and Moe's baby girl.

Slowly, Leigh's eyes moved back to Emma. The
woman was still watching her. How did she come to
raise Coral as her own granddaughter?

Suddenly, Leigh knew. Emma had been on that bus.

The old woman crept toward Leigh and sat down beside her. Instinctively, Leigh drew back. Emma leaned toward her, grabbed her arm. Her expression was menacing.

"You know, don't you? You figured it out. I see it on yo' face. How did you figure it out? What gave it away?"

"The olivine pendant. . . ."

"I shoulda thrown it away long time ago. I never let Ko'a wear it, but last night she decided to wear it anyway, without telling me. That girl—" Emma's hand tightened on Leigh's arm. "You're too *akamai*, too smart. I sent Derek to watch yo' bungalow that first night. I threw a rock through yo' aunt's window to get rid of you. It didn't work. But I'm gonna get rid of you now."

Leigh frowned at her, trying to comprehend what she meant. Emma grinned her toothless, crazed smile.

"You don't think I'll do it? When that bus crashed an' my baby granddaughter died, I had to have another baby to love. She was all I had. So I took Ko'a from Moekane. I beat his head with a rock so he wouldn't take Ko'a away from me. I saw yo' aunt, and I beat her head too, but she didn't die. She went away and left me and Ko'a alone. Ko'a is mine! And don't think I won't kill you too to keep yo' mouth shut!"

Leigh felt sick to her stomach. At that moment, she was intensely aware of the fiberglass gunwale under her hand, the drone of the boat's engine, the sight of Derek's set face as he maneuvered the tiller.

Derek. Was he in on this too? Why would he go along with something so desperate?

"Don't look at him fo' help," Emma said. "He wants you out of the way, just like me. He loves Ko'a, wants to marry her. I said he could one of these days. If Ko'a finds out she owns Wailani, you think she'd give Derek a second look? Long as she belongs to me, she belongs to Derek too. He knows that.

"I bet you wish Mr. Trowbridge or George would find you now, yeah?" Emma said. "But they don't want a nosy girl around either. Mr. Trowbridge grows enough *pakalolo* on government land to get everybody in Honolulu high. He doesn't think I know, but I do. I don't care. Long as he leaves me and Ko'a alone, he can do what he wants."

Leigh digested her words slowly. "And Kalani? I guess he's glad to get rid of me too, because of the marijuana—"

"Kalani don't have nothing to do wit' the *pakalolo*. He's trying to turn in Mr. Trowbridge."

"Then who's Malcolm?"

"Malcolm!" Emma spat out the name as if it had a foul taste in her mouth. "He thinks he's better than me! He'll make Ko'a think it too, if I don't keep her away from him!"

Leigh stared at her. There was a glint of madness in her eyes.

"Malcolm works for the government. He flies around the Big Island looking fo' crops of marijuana. He's been after Mr. Trowbridge fo' months, trying to catch him wit' his hands on the stuff. But Mr. Trowbridge is too smart. He told George to put some of the stuff in Kalani's boat, and then he called the police himself to make it look like Kalani was a dealer. I heard all this through the window when Malcolm sneaked in to see my Ko'a on the porch at night. He told her everything, and I heard. I told Derek to tell Mr. Trowbridge everything. I hoped he would get rid of Malcolm so he'd leave my Ko'a alone. But it didn't work yet. It will, though. I'll get rid of anybody trying to take my Ko'a away.'' She put her face in front of Leigh's. ''Anybody!''

Leigh looked off to the left. The coast of Hawaii slipped past them, rocky, dark, shrouded in mist, the cliffs looming ominously above. No one to see them, no one to rescue her from what was beginning to look like the end of her life.

''Where are you taking me?'' she demanded.

''A place where nobody can find you.''

''You're crazy, you know that? I'm not the only one who knows about you. My aunt's memory has come back. She remembers everything. She's probably already gone to the police to tell them about you. . . .''

Emma's low cackle was a distinctly unpleasant sound. ''You think I'm that stupid? I took care of her last night. Derek heard her tell Mr. Trowbridge how she remembers the bus accident, the baby, everything. They went outside, away from the party. Derek called me and told me. I went up there and hid, waiting. Derek called Mr. Trowbridge inside, and—wham!—I hit yo' aunt on the head and dragged her into the bushes. Mr. Trowbridge came back but couldn't find her. He thought she drove off someplace.

''When morning came, Derek and me put her in dis boat and took her up the coast, jus' like we're doing with her nosy niece.'' Emma gestured toward the land.

"The Hamakua coast is beautiful, no? Many valleys, steep valleys, no roads. Nobody goes down there. Nobody will find the woman who wants to take my Ko'a away from me."

"She wouldn't take her away from you!" Leigh grabbed the old woman's arm. "Coral loves you, she wouldn't leave you!"

"No!" Emma pushed her away. "I killed Moekane. Now I'm gonna finish the job."

Leigh stared at Emma. She could think of nothing else to say that might dissuade the woman. "Is—is she alive?" she asked tremulously.

"Las' time I saw her, she was." Emma looked earnest. "I won't kill her—Big Island will. The rains of Hamakua will kill her."

Leigh closed her eyes. *Hang on,* she told herself. *If you can just make it to Florence, you'll be able to save yourself and her too.* Somehow. . . .

She opened her eyes and glanced down at the spear gun on the floor of the boat. Emma's zoried feet came down firmly on the gun. "Oh, no, you don't," she said. "Don't even think about it."

Leigh looked away. She would wait for her chance. There had to be a way out of this.

She looked behind them. Through the mist, several miles down the coast, came the strong pinpoint flash of the lighthouse of Point Maka'u. Then she saw something else. It appeared for a moment, then dipped out of sight into a trough in the choppy ocean. A boat. It was a long way off, too far away for her to be able to tell which direction it was going, but instantly all her consciousness was riveted to that one small speck in the ocean. Someone was out there. She was not alone in the sea with a crazy old woman and a simple young man.

Leigh strained her eyes toward the place she had last seen the boat. She could not find it. Fingers of desperation drummed her insides. *Don't abandon me!* she cried silently. But the boat was gone. A gust of wind blew salt spray into her face, mocking her. Tears stung her eyes. She choked them back angrily. *They're not going to see me cry,* she vowed to herself.

Derek turned the prow toward the shoreline, and the stern of the boat swung around to follow its lead. It looked as if they were headed straight for the rocks. Leigh clutched the side of the boat and watched, wide-eyed, as the black lava cliffs loomed closer.

All at once the rocks opened up before them. A narrow passage, hidden among the folds of the cliffs, appeared. Derek guided the boat through it into a protected cove. Jagged cliffs rose almost straight up on all sides.

At the back of the cove, the cliffs parted in an ever-widening V toward the sky. Torrential waterfalls hurtled down the sides of the cliffs a thousand feet above them. As Leigh watched, a rain-soaked chunk of earth slid away from the face of the cliff and came tumbling down toward them. It hit the rocks at the edge of the water and exploded into thousands of pieces. Some of them splattered the boat and its passengers. Leigh winced. Emma grinned.

She whispered in Leigh's ear, "No one ever comes to Kapu Valley. No one can get away without a boat. If you stay here a long time, you get buried by falling cliff.'' She glanced up at the towering precipices and back at Leigh. ''If some smart girl who figured out too much disappeared, no one would think to look here. If they find a body—no bullet holes, no nothing. The cliffs killed the girl.''

Derek beached the boat with a thud and a jerk on the one small spot of sand among the craggy black rocks. Leigh scanned the black rocks at the water's edge. ''Where's Aunt Florence?''

''She's not here. You don't think I'd bring you to the same place as her? Together you could get away. Alone—never.''

''Then where is she?''

''Farther up the coast.'' Emma gestured north.

Desperately, Leigh turned to Derek. ''How can you help her do this? Do you think Coral would ever marry a murderer?''

For a moment he faltered. Then anger leaped into his eyes and Leigh knew she had said the wrong thing. He grabbed both her wrists and pulled her toward the side of the boat. Leigh screamed and struggled against him. She felt Emma's hands, surprisingly powerful, pushing her, lifting her from behind.

Derek climbed over the side of the boat and pulled Leigh with him. He hurled her away from him and she fell against a tall black lava boulder. The pumicelike surface of the rock scraped the palms of her hands, but she hardly noticed. She scrambled to her feet. Derek had already pushed the boat back into the water and was clambering up over the side. Leigh stumbled toward them.

"Don't leave me here!" she screamed. "You can't do this!"

And then she saw the other boat.

It had just entered the mouth of the cove and was moving toward them swiftly. Leigh had never seen a lovelier sight. She sobbed with relief and swung her arms in a wide arc over her head.

Emma saw the boat too. Her body went rigid. The craft came closer, gliding smoothly across the calm water of the bay. The single person in the boat sat in the stern, his hand on the tiller. It was Kalani.

Emma grabbed Derek's shirt. "Get him!" she shouted. "I'll take this boat, you take his! Throw him out with her!"

"No!" Leigh ran into the water mindlessly, trying to grab Emma's boat and hold it back somehow.

Kalani cut the motor and stood up as his boat approached Emma's. Derek jumped onto Kalani's boat as Kalani heaved a small anchor overboard. Derek shoved him. He almost fell into the water but caught himself in time. He turned and grabbed Derek, pinning the smaller man's arms to his sides. Derek kicked viciously at his legs. Kalani lifted him up and threw him off the boat.

Kalani scrambled out of the boat and splashed toward Leigh. She grabbed hold of him, sobbing.

"Stop!"

They both looked up. Emma was standing in her boat, her legs spread for balance. She held the spear gun like a rifle, pointed toward them. Behind her, Derek was climbing into Kalani's boat.

"You're staying right here—both of you!"

Leigh gasped and clutched Kalani. Above them, a huge chunk of cliff broke away and tumbled down toward them. They dropped to the sand and the rock sailed over their heads and splashed into the water, rocking both boats.

"Let's go!" Emma shouted to Derek. "I'm going to the house to pack and then I'm going to wait in the boat below Wailani. You go up and get Ko'a. Let's go!"

Helplessly, Leigh and Kalani watched as the two boats pulled away from them and headed toward the mouth of the cove. They became two white slivers on the silver-gray water of the cove; then they disappeared through the passage in the rocks.

Leigh held on to Kalani. She could feel the beating of his heart through his wet shirt, feel his hand on her hair.

From high above them came a deep rumbling. They both looked up. An enormous mass of earth slid a few feet down the face of the cliff and stopped. A handful of rocks showered down around them. He protected her head with his arms.

"We have to do something," he said. "When that piece of cliff falls, it's going to bury us. We can't stay here."

They looked around. In front of them was the water. Behind them, on all sides, were craggy black rocks ten to twelve feet high. Even if they could climb the rocks, they could not get far enough away to avoid the landslide. They were at the bottom of a funnel formed by the cliffs of Kapu Valley. There was no place to go.

"I'll have to swim for help," he said.

Leigh glanced up quickly. "What?" she cried. "Kalani, you'll never make it! You'll drown out there!"

"I think I can make it," he said as he pulled his shirt off over his head. "I have to try. If I don't, we'll be buried alive. If I get through, I can get help for you."

"Don't leave me! I don't want to be alone!"

He pulled her toward him and his arms went around her. His lips found hers and they were warm and strong and for a moment her fears dissolved. She wrapped her arms around his neck and thought that if he could go on kissing her, she would never fear anything again.

But he could not go on. He pulled her arms away from his neck. "I have to go." He started toward the water, then looked back over his shoulder. For a moment time froze as she looked at him, her Hawaiian prince, about to brave the fury of the Pacific. She would never see him again.

"I'll be back, Leigh," he said, reading her thoughts. "Hang on." He glanced up at the cliff and then turned and dove into the water.

His dark head broke the surface of the water a hundred yards away from shore. His powerful arms stroked over his head in an Australian crawl, drawing him closer to the mouth of the cove and farther away from Leigh. She watched until he disappeared through the pass in the rocks.

From overhead came another low rumble and a shower of pebbles and stones. She turned and huddled against the black lava rock. The wet, rough surface was cold under her hands. Her fingernails dug into the holes in the rock.

It began to rain again. Leigh bowed her head against the rock and closed her eyes.

## Chapter Thirteen

Leigh lost all sense of time. When she opened her eyes again, the gray light looked different, as if, behind the thick curtain of clouds, the sun had slipped closer to the horizon. She wondered what time it was. She did not want to be here alone when night fell.

Her fingers ached. They still clutched the craggy lava rock, and were so stiff she could hardly move them. She turned her hands over. The pads of her fingers were grayish-white and wrinkled with the salt water.

She looked up. A thousand feet up, the shifted plate of earth still clung to the face of the cliff. One more cloudburst, one more strong wind, would send it crashing down on top of her. Leigh was too drained to feel any of her initial terror. If it fell, she simply didn't want to see it coming.

She turned to look out at the cove. Its surface was silver and mirrorlike, reflecting the clouded sky and the sheer cliffs. Kalani had swum across that cove a lifetime ago. He could not possibly have made it through the jagged rocks and pounding waves. And yet he had risked it to save her.

She looked down at the patch of sand on which she stood. It looked different now. Bigger. There was more sand.

Her eyes followed the stretch of sand along the edge of the cove. There had been no sand there when she was first thrown onto this little patch—she was sure of it. Now, if she wanted to, she could walk all the way to the far edge of the cove.

Then she realized what had happened. It was low tide. It had sucked the ocean away from the shore just enough to save her.

Leigh made her way around the rocks on the narrow, wet strip of sand to the far side of the cove. She clambered up onto a lava rock, cutting her toes on the rough edges. But when she reached the top and sat down, she would be out of the water when the tide came back in.

From her perch on the rock she looked back toward where she had been. The rock she had clung to looked puny at the base of the colossal cliff that had threatened to bury her. The sheet of earth still hung on precariously. If it fell now, she would be pelted with stones, but at least she had a chance.

Where was Aunt Florence? Was she still alive? Was she, too, on the floor of a valley that threatened to bury her alive? *Hang on, Aunt Florence,* Leigh thought, echoing Kalani's words to her.

Leigh heard a low rumbling. She stared up at the cliff. The chunk of earth hung motionless. She listened. It was growing stronger. It came from the sky. Thunder. But no, it was too prolonged. Too regular. As it grew nearer, the sound resolved into the beat-beat-beat of a helicopter.

Instinctively, fear seized her and she cowered down against the rock. But as the pontooned helicopter whirled into view over the tops of the cliffs, she was staggered with relief. The helicopter slowed, swung around, and dropped down toward her.

Leigh's eyes never left it. Her every nerve was taut, expectant. Two people were in the helicopter. She caught a glimpse of the pilot as he looked for a place to land. It was Malcolm.

The helicopter swung out over the cove and hovered there, the surface of the water ruffling under the wind of the propeller. Then, with the daintiness of a lady alighting from a carriage, the pontoons set down in the water.

The door opened. Kalani climbed out. Waist-deep in water, he waded toward Leigh on the rock.

She scrambled down off the rock, ignoring the numerous scrapes and cuts she inflicted on herself, and slogged through the water toward him. Kalani's face was set in an expressionless mask, but as Leigh reached him and his arms went around her, she knew that behind the mask was the Kalani who loved her, who had risked his life for her.

"You're alive," she whispered rather unnecessarily. "You made it."

He lifted her up in his arms and carried her across the water to the open door of the waiting helicopter. He passed her in and she plunked into a seat. She turned to look at Malcolm.

He greeted her with a wry, quirky smile, partially concealed by the mouthpiece of the headset he wore.

Leigh laughed at the irony of it. "I never thought I'd say this, Malcolm Yamashiro, but am I glad to see you!" Her smile faded. "Listen, we have to get to Aunt Florence fast! I hope she isn't. . . ."

"Do you know where she is?"

"Emma took her to another valley farther up the coast."

"Hang on."

Kalani climbed into the helicopter and closed the door. With a thump and a whir Malcolm lifted the helicopter off the water and into the air.

Leigh caught her breath as her stomach plunged. She looked out the window and saw Kapu Valley drop away below them. As she watched, the sheet of earth slid and tumbled down to the rocks of the cove with a tremendous splash. The rock she had clung to for so long was buried by the landslide.

Leigh glanced at Malcolm. She took in the complicated control board in front of him, the gun in the holster at his hip, the insignia on his cap that identified him as a member of a government drug control unit.

"You could have told me," she said. "It would have saved me a lot of panic."

"We couldn't trust you enough to tell you," Malcolm said. "At first we thought you might be working with them. You were a guest of Simon's, after all, and you were very friendly with George Honua. I always meant to apologize for my behavior on the plane, by the way. The pendant you were wearing looked just like one of Coral's. I was just surprised."

Leigh looked at Kalani. They would tell Malcolm about the pendant later. Now hardly seemed the time. ''What about you?'' she asked Kalani. ''Are you working for the government too?''

Kalani glanced past her at Malcolm. He looked troubled.

''No,'' Malcolm said. ''He's just helping us out. He was brought into this against his will. Simon tried to pin the drug business on him, and the only way he could avoid a smuggling conviction was to help us catch Simon. It's hard when you're up against your own grandfather.''

''So you know about that.''

''I had to. Every detail is important in a case like this. Kalani and I have become pretty good friends through it all.''

Kalani stared out at the passing coastline.

Green cliffs and deep gorges passed beneath them. As another valley opened up below, Malcolm dropped the helicopter down into its verdant depths. The aircraft hovered a few feet above the surface of the water as they scanned the shoreline. Malcolm put the binoculars to his eyes.

''I don't see anything,'' he said. ''Do you know what color she was wearing?''

''Maybe peach chiffon.''

Another few tense minutes passed. ''I don't see her,'' he repeated as he lifted the helicopter up and away. ''We'll try the next valley.''

They followed the series of valleys up the coast. With each disappointment Leigh grew more hopeless. Florence had been alone out here since early this morning; she could have been swept away by the high tide or fallen from the rocks trying to climb to safety. *Aunt Florence, your daughter is alive, you can't die now. . . .*

"I see her!" Malcolm exclaimed. He pointed. Leigh's eyes followed his finger to a place among the dense jungle growth that edged a rocky beach. Under the green fronds of an immense fern Leigh spotted the pale peach color of Florence's evening gown. "I see her too! She's down there!"

Malcolm swooped the helicopter down to the rocky beach and landed. Leigh and Kalani climbed out and ran toward Florence.

Her evening gown was twisted, wet, streaked with mud. Her eyes were closed, her face haggard. She looked dead.

"Aunt Florence!"

The woman stirred. She looked up. "Leigh! Oh, Leigh. . . ." She tried to stand up, but cramped, cold muscles failed her and she fell to the ground. Kalani scooped her up and her head lolled against his shoulder.

They laid her in the back of the helicopter with a first-aid pillow under her head. Her eyes fluttered and closed with fatigue. Malcolm gave them a blanket to put over her. They lifted away toward the south.

"No wonder I couldn't find her," Kalani said. "After I left you at the bungalow, I took my boat down the coast in the other direction. I thought she and Simon might be somewhere between here and Hilo."

"Simon and George showed up at the bungalow after you left. I hid from them in the closet. I heard them talking about you and Malcolm—and me. I was stupid enough to tell George about what I overheard at the party last week.''

Malcolm pounced on her words. ''What did you tell him?''

''That you and Kalani were going to be at the pickup on Saturday.''

''What did they say?''

''They've changed the pickup to tonight.''

There was a silence as the two men exchanged glances. ''Are you sure?'' Kalani asked.

''One way to find out,'' Malcolm said. ''See if Simon has his red flag flying. That's his signal to the boat.''

''What about Emma?'' Leigh asked. ''Someone has to stop her.''

''We can't call the police yet,'' Malcolm said. ''If Simon sees them anywhere in the vicinity, it'll scare him off and we won't bag him. Emma won't go anywhere for a while. She thinks she's rid of all of you. And there's Coral.'' His voice softened. ''She won't run off and leave her behind.''

''No,'' Leigh agreed. ''But we heard her tell Derek she was going to go home and pack and wait for him in the boat below Wailani. Derek's going to get Coral, and they're all leaving in the boat. If we don't do something soon, they'll be gone.''

Malcolm's face went slack. Leigh glimpsed again the vulnerable look she had seen at the party. He flicked a switch on the control panel.

''We'll take care of it as soon as possible. Right now I have to radio this new information to my unit.

They'd better be ready in case a pickup does go down tonight.''

Leigh glanced out the large bubble window of the helicopter. The gray daylight had faded into black-velvet evening. A few scattered lights twinkled down the coast. In the darkness the phosphorescence of the breakers traced a ghostly line along the shore.

Beside her Kalani suddenly sat forward in his seat. He stared ahead with narrowed eyes.

"What is it?" she asked.

He pointed. "I see lights in the cove at Wailani. I think there's a boat."

Malcolm interrupted his radio communication. He picked up the binoculars and trained them toward the lights at the cove.

"They're there," he said into the radio. "The exchange must be happening right now." He glanced at Leigh and Kalani. "Hold on. I'm going in."

The helicopter zoomed down toward the cove. Malcolm switched on a powerful searchlight. Abruptly, the cove was bathed in light.

Four men stared up at them, their mouths agape. Two of them scrambled over the rocks to a waiting boat. The other two climbed the low sea cliff to the level ground above and started to run. The boat's engines fired up and the bow of the boat swung around toward open water. The helicopter circled the boat as Malcolm spoke through the public-address system.

"Return to shore. Return to shore. You are under arrest. Do not attempt to escape."

A bullet cracked the windshield of the helicopter. Kalani pulled Leigh toward him. Malcolm lifted the aircraft in an attempt to get it out of firing range and spoke into the radio. ''Exchange is already completed. Boat is headed east by southeast at approximately ten knots. Two suspects are escaping on foot from the scene. They are armed.''

A man's voice crackled over the radio. ''On our way to intercept vessel. Stay with other suspects.''

The helicopter turned and headed toward the fleeing men. When they heard the helicopter above them, they shielded their heads with their arms and stumbled on.

''Halt!'' Malcolm commanded through the public-address system. He drew his gun from its holster and fired a warning shot out the side window.

The two men on the ground stopped and turned with their hands up. They were Simon and George.

Malcolm landed the helicopter and shut down the motor. ''Wait here,'' he said to Kalani, and climbed out.

He advanced toward the two men with his handgun aimed at them. ''Stay where you are,'' he said.

George made a move to run. Malcolm whipped the gun toward him and he stopped. Kalani leaped out of the helicopter.

''I'm authorized to use this,'' Malcolm said to George. ''Don't think I won't. Kalani, get back.''

''You might need me,'' Kalani said firmly.

''He won't do you any good!''

Everyone turned. Emma stood at the edge of the sea cliff. Her lower legs were wet, as if she had just waded through water. In her hand she held a gun, which she pointed at the group. It looked like the gun Leigh had found in Simon's desk.

Emma advanced on the small group before her. "Drop dat gun, now!" She waved the pistol menacingly. Malcolm tossed his gun to the ground. Emma scooped it up. She looked at Simon and George. "You both can come with us. My boat is waiting over there. We can all get away together! They'll never find us."

George did not wait for another invitation. He bolted in the direction Emma had indicated, down the sea cliff toward the place where the boat waited unseen. Simon, however, did not move.

"What are you going to do?" he asked her.

"What I should have done long time ago! I'm gonna get rid of these troublemakers!"

"Leave them," Simon said. "I'm willing to take my chances with drug smuggling, but not with murder. Let's go."

"You crazy? Malcolm's gonna throw you in jail fo' the rest of yo' life because of all that *pakalolo* you grow and sell. This is your chance to get away! What do they mean to you?"

"Some of them mean a lot to me, Emma."

"Tutu, what are you doing?"

Emma whirled around. Coral and Derek hurried down the path from Wailani. Coral was still dressed in her black uniform and white apron. Her steps slowed when she saw the gun in Emma's hand. She looked at the old woman, waiting for an answer.

Emma's hand wavered. Shame struggled with rage in her face. "Derek, take her down to the boat!" she snapped.

Derek tried to drag Coral toward the sea cliff, but

she angrily shook free of him. "Malcolm—" she began.

"Go on! This boy is no good. All these people are no good! They tried to take you away from me. You love yo' tutu, no? All right, then. Get in the boat. Me and Derek will take care of you."

Leigh scrambled out of the helicopter. "Coral, don't go! She isn't really your grandmother! She killed your father when you were a baby!"

"Shut your mouth!" Emma screamed, and pointed the gun at Leigh. Leigh stopped in her tracks. "You stupid girl! I won't let you ruin everything! Shut up or I'll shoot you dead!"

Coral stared at Leigh. A puzzled frown creased her forehead and she looked at Emma. "What did she mean, Tutu? Aren't you my grandmother?"

"Of course! I told you, they're trying to take you away from me. Don't listen! Now go!"

"Leigh?"

It was Florence. She was awake, bleary-eyed and disheveled, leaning out of the helicopter door. Emma's mouth fell open.

"Florence!" Astonished, Simon started toward the helicopter. Then he stopped himself.

Leigh turned to Coral. "Do something! She's your mother. Aunt Florence is your mother!"

Everyone stared at Leigh.

"It's true!" she cried. "Why do you think Emma wants to kill her? Just like she killed Moe Akina!"

A gunshot exploded in the air. The bullet ricocheted off the helicopter's propeller shaft. Terrified, Florence fell back into the helicopter. Coral screamed and jumped at Emma. Simon came at her from the other side and together they wrenched the gun out of Emma's hands. Emma stumbled backward. She glared at Coral.

"How can you do this to me? I took care of you all yo' life! I love you, Ko'a! Why don't you love me?"

"I do love you! That's why I'm doing this!"

They stared at each other, old woman and young, one sad but purposeful, the other wild-eyed with rage and madness. Coral turned to Malcolm and handed his gun back to him.

From far off in the night came a new sound, one that was by now familiar to Leigh. She looked up. A helicopter was approaching.

"Let's get out of here!" Simon shouted. He and Emma and Derek made a break for the sea cliff. Coral started after them.

"Tutu—"

"Coral! Stay back!" Malcolm shouted, and when she obeyed, he fired two shots at Simon. The second caught him in the leg and he stumbled and fell over the sea cliff. Emma and Derek had already disappeared.

"Simon!" Florence screamed.

The lights of the helicopter came into view overhead. Its blinding searchlight came on and swept the group on the ground as the helicopter slowly circled. Malcolm signaled to them. The searchlight swept the water surrounding the point.

The light caught and held Emma's boat as it put out to sea. Emma was in the stern, guiding the tiller. George and Derek sat in front of her and they looked up at the helicopter as the pilot called to them to return to shore. Emma did not. She kept her eyes straight ahead as the boat bounded over the swells, making for the open sea beyond the rocks.

The huge black lava rocks loomed directly ahead of them. George and Derek shouted at Emma but she did not swerve. She pressed the boat toward the rocks with gathering speed. The helicopter pilot followed overhead, calling repeated warnings. Derek and George scrambled to their feet and dove overboard.

Emma and the boat plummeted into the rocks. The boat burst apart, shards of white fiberglass flashing into the water. The gasoline-filled engine exploded and orange flames blossomed into the black night.

Slowly, the remains of the boat sank into the sea.

Two hours later, Leigh sat in a chair in the living room of Kalani's house, wrapped in a blanket, sipping a cup of coffee. The cuts and scratches on her hands and legs throbbed. The coffee warmed the chill off her body and she slowly relaxed into the cushioned comfort of the chair.

The rescue team from the helicopter had pulled Simon, injured but alive, out of the rocks into which he had fallen. He had been taken to the hospital in Kamuela under police custody. The team had also fished George and Derek out of the ocean and they had been taken to Kamuela for questioning. Emma's body had not been found.

Florence sat on the couch near Leigh. Coral sat on the couch beside Florence, her hands clasped around her knees. She seemed amazingly calm for what she had just been through. The police had finished questioning her only a moment ago and were now off in the corner, speaking in low tones with Malcolm. Perhaps, Leigh thought, all of this would come crashing in on her later.

Coral watched Florence take a sip of her coffee and set the cup down on the table in front of them. When Florence looked at her, Coral smiled but said nothing. Florence reached up as if to stroke Coral's hair, but she paused, hesitated, and lowered her hand.

"Your father and I named you Elizabeth," she said. "But Coral suits you better. I like it." She studied the girl's face. "Now that I look at you I see a lot of Moekane—your father—in you. And some of myself too."

Coral's thickly lashed eyes fluttered. She drew back ever so slightly. *Too much has happened too soon,* Leigh thought. *She can't accept it all yet.*

Florence seemed to sense it too. "I guess you're not ready to hear that," she said. "I'm sorry about your grandmother."

"Thank you. I'm sorry, too, for what she did to you all those years ago."

Florence nodded, gingerly patted Coral's knee, and fell silent.

The front door opened and Kalani came into the house, followed by his father and a police officer. The three of them joined the conference in the corner with Malcolm and the other policemen. There were more questions asked, statements made, notes taken, and then the officers left.

Kalani and Malcolm came across the room to where the three women were seated. Florence gazed up at Kalani.

"So you're Sharon's son," she said. "Your mother was the dearest friend I ever had, you know." She threw a knowing look at her niece. "He's a beautiful young man, Leigh. If this one doesn't take your breath away, I've lost all hope for you."

Leigh gazed at Kalani. His big dark eyes met hers. "There's hope for me yet, Aunt Florence," she said.

A short while later Leigh and Kalani slipped quietly out of the house. The night air was thick and warm. It had stopped raining, and overhead the clouds were breaking apart and the moon peeked through the mist.

"My father will be here day after tomorrow," Leigh said. "I just remembered."

There was a silence beside her. "Will you be going home with him?"

"No. Not now. He was afraid I'd have some trouble with Aunt Florence, but now that everything's settled I intend to finish my vacation. But I'm glad he'll be able to meet you."

Kalani looked out at the night. "Will your aunt be moving to Hawaii?"

"Probably. She'll want to be where Coral is, and now that Coral owns Wailani. . . ."

"What about you?"

Leigh looked up into Kalani's face. His eye caught the gleam of the moon as it broke through the clouds.

"What about me?" she whispered.

He slid his hand under her hair, along the side of her neck. His hand was warm and strong and thrilling. "You can't leave," he said. "Not now. Not even in two weeks."

"But I have to go back and finish law school. And

I told Townsend & Kohler I'd be back. I don't know
how they'll ever get along without me—"

His warm lips came down over hers. She melted
into his arms. He filled her senses, her thoughts, her
world. *Kalani,* she thought. *I can't believe I've found
you.*

"I'm the one who can't get along without you," he
said as he leaned his forehead against hers. His voice
was husky with emotion. "Since the day I first saw
you there's been this great hollow aching in me that
only you can fill. Don't leave me here alone, Leigh.
Marry me and be my love."

Leigh looked into his eyes. All at once it became
crystal-clear to her what she wanted to do with her
life. She wanted to graduate from law school and go
into practice. As Mrs. Kalani Akina. *Come to me,
enfold me in your arms, let me feel your hand beneath
my neck. For on this day I join my life to yours. . . .*

"Life wouldn't be worth living any other way," she
said.

They both smiled. Leigh turned her head and looked
through the window into the living room. Malcolm was
saying something to Coral. Tears streamed down her
face. Suddenly she jumped off the couch and threw
her arms around him. Then she turned and embraced
Florence. Florence returned the embrace, and they re-
mained locked in each other's arms for a long time.

Leigh felt Kalani's hand stroke her hair. She turned
and looked out at the night.

Out in the darkness, the beam of the lighthouse at
Point Maka'u flashed across the night and disappeared.